London Comfort

From Hollywood to the White House: An American Idol's Dangerous Real World Adventure

Henry E. Scott

D1738423

The Pine Forest Press
Los Angeles, CA
www.thepineforestpress.com

All of the characters in this book are fictitious except for those actual
national political figures who are parodied and identified by name.

ISBN: 1469931338
ISBN-13: 978-1469931333

DEDICATION

This book is dedicated to Michele Bachman, Herman Cain, Newt Gingrich, Ron Paul, Rick Perry, Mitt Romney, and Rick Santorum, whose zany campaigns for the Republican presidential nomination have made credible the incredible story that follows.

London Comfort

From Hollywood to the White House: An American Idol's Dangerous Real World Adventure

CHAPTER 1

SATURDAY, FEBRUARY 15
405 FREEWAY
WILSHIRE BLVD EXIT
LOS ANGELES, CA

"Oh fuck!"

The flashing red and blue light penetrated the tinted windows of London Comfort's Bentley GT, bouncing off her rear view mirror, the inside of the windshield, and the cover of the speedometer, which read seventy-five miles per hour. It was followed in less than a second by the low "mwah-mwah" of a siren that grew louder and louder and louder until the sound smothered the beat of Theodis Ealey's "Stand Up In It" that blared from the speakers.

"Oh, fuck! Oh, fuck! Oh, fuck!"

As she slowed down and steered the car to the narrow edge of the 405, London ran through her mental checklist. Drugs? Nothing in the car, she was sure of that, although she had done two lines at Jason's party. Booze? She'd had only three drinks. She was a girl who could hold her liquor. So no worries about

1

touching her nose with her eyes closed. Still, what a drag this was going to be. If she hadn't been so determined to bust Jason's balls, she would have stayed at the party, spent the night with him, and she wouldn't be going through this crap. But she'd promised herself that until he gave up that video of her, Jason wasn't getting any more nooky from London. She came to a stop, turned off the ignition, and let out a deep sigh. Maybe at least the cop would be hot. She'd seen a movie where the cop who stopped a girl ended up in the sack with her. She did have this uniform fantasy. But those CHiPS guys looked like they'd spent too much time at Krispy Kreme. Real life was disappointing like that. On the other hand, those UPS guys always turned her on. London still had fantasies about what brown could do for her.

Finally, the siren died, and London looked into the rear view mirror. He had just stepped out of the cruiser, and in the oncoming headlights he was looking good. Just maybe she'd get out of this if her smile said innocent and her eyes said sexy and she touched his hand longingly as she passed over her license.

"Good evening, ma'am. Can I see your license and registration?"

He was maybe thirty. Thick, hairy forearms. Thick, dark eyebrows. A square jaw and low forehead. Just the sort of Neanderthal man that turned her on. Just the sort of Neanderthal man that was impossible to find at the clubs and parties where she hung out. She fished in her Birkin for her wallet, extracted her license, and handed it to him, making sure to caress his palm ever so slightly as she did. He started, but not in a bad way.

"Let me find my registration." she said.

She stretched over toward the glove compartment on her right, conscious that her butt, one of her best features according to the gossip columnists, was elevated off the seat. She found the leather portfolio with all of the car papers and handed it him with a polite smile.

"What was I doing wrong, officer?"

"Well, ma'am, you were talking on your cell phone a few

miles back, and you weren't wearing your seatbelt, and you were doing seventy five miles an hour in a sixty five zone. Now, you stay right here while I go back to my vehicle for a moment."

He walked away, and she looked at her watch and sighed. Five a.m. and in eight hours she had to be at the Ivy for lunch with her agent and that woman from Warnaco. A London Comfort lingerie line! She didn't even wear panties! She drummed her fingers on the steering wheel and looked into the rear view mirror. He was still talking on his walkie-talkie or whatever. She needed to pee. She needed to sleep. She needed to get this over with and go home. And now what's this? Another cruiser is pulling up? Don't these people have real work to do?

Suddenly her cave man was back at her window, this time accompanied by a black woman, if you could call her a woman, in a uniform that looked a lot like his. Her breasts drooped down over her waist. She wore a huge phallic nightstick on her belt. Her hair was cropped tight. When she got really close, London couldn't believe the size of her hands.

"Ma'am, would you step out of the car please?" she said. "We're going to have to take you in."

"Take me in? Officer, for what? What do you mean take me in? Can't I just get my ticket and go home? Oh my God! What is happening?"

Cro Magnon man spoke up.

"Ma'am, we're placing you under arrest for driving seventy-five in a sixty-five-mile-per-hour zone, for driving without wearing a seatbelt, for talking on a cell phone while driving, and for driving while your license is suspended. Ma'am, you have the right to an attorney. If you cannot afford one, one will be appointed for you. You have the right to remain silent. Anything you say may be used against you in a court of law. Do you understand your rights ma'am?"

London nodded, biting her lip to keep from crying. She stepped out of the car onto the broken pavement, snapping the heel off one of her Roger Viviers in the process. Then the woman cop asked her to turn around and put her hands behind her back.

3

"You're going to handcuff me? Why are you going to handcuff me? I can't believe this!"

As the metal cuffs closed around her wrists and locked with a clink, London let go. Tears streamed down her face, washing her eyeliner with them, and a warm stream of urine trickled down the inside of her left leg. With a quick shove, the woman cop bobbed London's head down as she pushed her into the back seat of the waiting cruiser. The door closed with a tinny slam that London noticed was nothing like the solid clunk of her Bentley. In just seconds, lights flashing, they were off.

London twisted to get comfortable on the vinyl seat, made clammy by the wet spot on the back of her skirt.

"You okay honey?" asked the woman cop.

They handcuff her hands behind her back, and they want to know if she's okay? London didn't respond. It seemed like only a few minutes had passed when they pulled off the highway and twisted and turned down blocks dotted with small houses and anchored by corners where groups of black and brown men stared sullenly at the police car. Suddenly they stopped in front of a bland three- or four-story building whose sign identified it as the Century Regional Detention Facility. It looked to London like one of those cheap hotels her father had managed when he first came to the United States from Saudi Arabia — before he made his fortune, and before he changed his last name to Comfort in what London's agent had called a brilliant piece of branding.

The drive was full of cars. Suddenly London realized why. Photographers! How did they know she was going to be there? How did they know what was going on?

"Oh, fuck!"

It's not like she wasn't used to photographers. God knows, they followed her practically everywhere. They were one reason her father had nagged her to get her own driver and make sure she had a security guy with her at all times. But London liked to drive. London liked to be in control. London liked being photographed. She'd learned to keep her head high and smile demurely as she walked through a sea of flashes. Tobias, her makeup artist, had even created a special foundation for her that he claimed was ideal for a face constantly assaulted by bright light. London, however, had never thought about how she'd handle a situation like this. She'd seen people on TV and in magazines who were arrested and walked into courthouses and jails with jackets over their heads. That looked so pitiful, so lame. London's impulse was to walk in with a regal pose, not smiling exactly, but not looking frightened or sad either. On the other hand, her makeup had to be a mess. She was missing a heel on one of her shoes. There was that wet spot on her skirt. What would that look like in US Weekly?

As if she had been reading London's mind, the woman cop spoke up.

"Keep your head high honey," she said. "Don't let 'em see you crying. Don't let 'em see you looking scared. Don't act like you got something to be ashamed of."

For a moment, London was ashamed. This woman was being nice to her, while London had been thinking she was so impossibly pathetic and ugly. She smiled at the woman, who smiled back. There was beauty hidden under that ugly blue uniform.

"Thanks," she said, slipping off the other Roger Vivier so she could walk comfortably. "I will."

CHAPTER 2

SATURDAY, FEBRUARY 15
SOMEWHERE IN THE TOBA KAKAR MOUNTAINS, PAKISTAN

"Oh, neik!"

Abdullah looked quickly outside his tent. He was relieved that none of his bodyguards seemed to be within earshot. His men knew he had a temper, having received many a stern rebuke invoking the Prophet's name. Still, it wouldn't do to be heard using that sort of profanity.

There was reason to be angry. At night, the temperature was twenty-five degrees, and during the day it was hot, with alternating torrents of dust and rain that blew through even the tiniest holes in a man's tent. Abdullah was dirty. Abdullah was wet. Abdullah was tired. Now, after learning that the latest plan to wreak terror on the Great Satan had come to naught, Abdullah was pissed.

It wasn't easy trying to top 9/11. But Abdullah knew he had to try. He knew that both narcissistic American capitalists and fanatically devout Muslims shared one thing — a short attention span. He knew what the Americans were thinking: "Sure you Muslims blew up the Twin Towers. But we killed bin Laden. What have you done lately?" And his Muslim brothers, the dwindling number of whom weren't spending all their time with video games and cell phone apps? Well if Abdullah and his men didn't do something big soon, they'd find someone who would. Maybe it was paranoia, but lately when Abdullah walked around his compound some of his men looked more like possible rivals than supporters. Having majored in marketing at King Abdul-Aziz University in Jeddah, he knew Abdullah bin-Salem's reputation was only as good as his last bombing. Routine acts of terror in Muslim countries — a car bombing in Baghdad, a market in flames in Beirut — barely rated thirty seconds on Al Jazeera these days. No, Abdullah need to take his campaign back to the heart of infidel culture, and in a big way. That was increasingly hard to do, witness the latest efforts of Ahmed Azhar, Abdullah's nephew, and one of only a handful of friends he was sure he could trust. Ahmed, having studied at Mississippi State University, spoke English with a Southern accent — a characteristic that led airport security staffers to see him as a rube rather than a rebel. With that, and a career as a model, he could slip into and out of the United States and Europe without arousing suspicion.

Abdullah crumpled in his hand the latest chronicle of failure. One hundred thousand dollars and six months spent recruiting a team of four young men to drive a pickup loaded with fertilizer-based explosives through the front doors of the biggest Wal-Mart in Kansas. The problem was the decadence of the United States. According to Ahmed, it was impossible to lure young men to the cause of Allah with the promise of martyrdom in heaven surrounded by seven young virgins. According to Ahmed, there were no female virgins in America over the age of fifteen, and young men didn't mind. Instead they, or so Ahmed said, preferred girls with experience. The team Ahmed had recruited in Kansas seemed promising at first, although not that religious. They were computer geeks — nerds the Americans called them. One of them reportedly spent eight hours a day editing submissions on Wikipedia (where Abdullah had spent more than a few hours correcting some of the more outrageous errors in his biography). Another spent his out-of-school hours on something called Second Life, a virtual community, whatever that was. The other two were website programmers. Abdullah had seen pictures of them. While one of them looked like the star of a teen girl movie, the others three were fat with faces dotted with acne and bad haircuts. Those boys were not going to get laid without some divine help. Ahmed had recruited the Kansas team at a madrassa in Kansas City. Ahmed's initiative pleased Abdullah. While he loved Ahmed like a son, he had to admit he shared some of his friends' concerns about his obsession with fashion and his reluctance to accept the wife that had been offered him. So he was relieved to hear that while Ahmed was in Kansas City to model for an underwear show at Neiman Marcus, he also was doing Allah's work, visiting the local madrassa and the local mosque to recruit some help. That's where Ahmed had met Hassan, the handsome young man who was a dead ringer for Wael kfoury in his younger days, a star to whom Ahmed was often compared.

Ahmed had offered to take Hassan and his friends to see a movie called "Primer," apparently a geek masterpiece, at a local college film festival. After that it was flights by Ahmed back and forth from New York, where he frequently modeled for Calvin Klein, to talk with the young men about the Prophet and the insidiousness of American culture. Slowly he introduced the idea that these boys could do something about it. Martyrdom was always a tough sell. But, Ahmed told Abdullah, these boys lived such virtual lives that giving up real life hardly would matter. The clincher was the seven virgins, or a total of twenty-eight, given that all four boys were needed for this plot, and also Ahmed's promise of eternal work on a new social community that the Prophet was building on the Web. Okay, so that wasn't exactly something one would find in the Koran, but Abdullah understood that an Islamic revolution required unusual measures that Allah would forgive.

Finally, everything was set. Abdullah's lieutenants alerted a friendly correspondent at Al Jazeera that there would be some big news on July 4, and it wouldn't be the Macy's fireworks and a patriotic speech by the ruler of the Great Satan. Abdullah had even trimmed his beard a little and washed up for the video his men were planning to make. And then — nothing happened.

Hassan, Ahmed said, had "gotten lucky," as the Americans described it. When he was supposed to have been driving the pickup, the boy had been at home trolling MySpace, an explanation Abdullah didn't really understand. There Hassan met a young American girl of loose morals who happened to be into Arab guys. The boy had gotten laid. Suddenly seven young virgins in heaven looked like a bunch of birds in the bush compared to a very randy bird who was eating out of Hassan's handsome hand.

Abdullah was furious. Abdullah was discouraged. What do you do in a society where sex is so easy that even the promise of seven young virgins in Heaven isn't enough? It was a promise that was beginning to lose its appeal in the Middle East as well, what with word getting around that the seven young virgins was a mistranslation of a Koranic promise of seven white raisins, which, Abdullah knew, had been as rare a treat as virgins in the Prophet's time.

"Khatraa! Khatraa! Khatraa!"

Abdullah's brief indulgence in self-pity was over. The screams of danger were quickly followed by the whistling sound of a missile, then an explosion. He stepped out of his tent to find his men running to their various vehicles. Two of them grabbed him by the arms and hoisted him into a jeep. It was a drone, they said. The Americans had found them. They sped along a bumpy and narrow path, sending up clouds of dust, in search of an overhang that a drone's missile couldn't pierce. Abdullah turned to look behind. A column of smoke was arising from the middle of his encampment of thirty tents, many of which were on fire. With luck, they'd be able to return later to retrieve whatever belongings had survived. Luck, however, was in short supply these days. Abdullah resigned himself to the possibility that they would be starting over, sleeping in their jeeps and trucks with no protection from the sun and rain and cold and dirt until they managed to scrounge some new supplies.

The next morning Abdullah and a dozen of his men started to make their wary way back to the camp. Against the advice of his senior lieutenants, he had situated it in an open yet inconveniently remote area, with a Pakistani general's assurance that the Americans never would find them there. He watched his men arguing and gesturing among themselves. From the way they fell silent when he approached, it was clear they were talking about that decision and him. They were wet and hungry and demoralized. A count the night before had turned up a dozen missing, all now martyrs in Allah's cause.

They drove in their jeeps out of the cold mountain shadows and into the brilliant desert sun. Down below, Abdullah could see what remained of the camp, where the tattered canvas of the remaining tents flapped gently in the light breeze like white flags signaling surrender. They stopped first at the site where the drone's missile had landed to pay tribute to their martyred brothers. Then Abdullah and his men broke down the surviving tents. His had survived, and he was relieved to find the leather pouch that contained his most important and private possessions.

In less than two hours they were back in the dark mountain shadows, erecting the tents they had rescued. The roar of several cooking fires and the clatter of pots and pans injected some life into what had been a deadly quiet scene the night before. At one point Abdullah even thought he heard laughter. After dinner, he made a speech in which he attempted to rouse his men to revenge, reminding them that martyrdom was a great privilege. Then he crawled back into his tent for some reflection. He was surrounded by two dozen fellow fighters. Yet he felt alone. He was reviled in the Western media as the most dangerous man in the world. Yet he felt impotent.

Abdullah was beginning to think young Hassan had been wise to choose the assurance of sex in Kansas over the possibility of martyrdom in Heaven. After all, he had gambled everything to rid the world of infidels and bring Allah's grace and glory to earth. But it wasn't working out — the aborted Kansas bombing had been one in a string of failures. And unlike Hassan, Abdullah hadn't been with a woman in a long time. That was to be expected, he realized, given that he spent his days in a tent in the Pakistani mountains, surrounded by his mujahideen supporters. Back in the day, he recalled, with a chuckle to himself, he'd had more than his share of virgins and women of more accomplishment. As the first son of the fourth wife of the wealthiest real estate developer in Jeddah, Abdullah was seen as quite a catch. He became expert at divining what lay underneath those damned burkas, the head-to-toe black garments that he hated as a young man but now had to support for religious reasons.

Abdullah also got to experience sex with the infidels. When he finished college, he was given a passport and an allowance that gave him the chance to explore Beirut and Istanbul, and later Paris and London and Berlin. For a while, he had considered staying in Paris to run a branch of his father's business. He was almost ashamed to remember how much he had enjoyed that city. There was a club called Cleopatra where he had been a regular. At Cleopatra, Abdullah experienced sins he hadn't even imagined growing up in Saudi Arabia. He still didn't understand the allure of the latex bodysuits that so many of Cleopatra's female patrons wore. The restaurant served food that was remarkably pedestrian for a city such as Paris. But then one didn't go to Cleopatra to eat. More important appetites were sated in a suite of rooms behind the bar, where black leather tables and divans supported all manner of public sex. His family wealth and social standing, invisible in that atmosphere, did nothing for Abdullah. His six-foot-five height and long beard, which woman said tickled in the most amazing way, were what got him laid.

His father, however, called him home. There he found a wife waiting for him, and a job in the family business. Adara, the daughter of one of his father's business partners, certainly was the virgin her name would suggest. The problem was that she never learned to enjoy sex. After a year of unrestrained coupling in Paris, Abdullah found the always-tentative intercourse with his wife a disappointment. The job wasn't much better. His father, determined not to show undue favoritism at so early an age to one of his dozen sons, detailed him to a division that built housing for immigrant workers. Abdullah's job was site manager, a task that kept him in the hot sun overseeing inconsequential projects and incompetent émigrés. Most of the time, he sat in his trailer and read. The story, as his PR firm later spun it, is that he rediscovered the Koran and developed his revolutionary fervor during those long days in that trailer. In fact, it was an article in an old issue of Time magazine, probably left behind by a Halliburton contractor, that really launched Abdullah on his jihad. "Enterprising Evangelism" described in detail the influence that television preachers such as Jim Bakker and Jimmy Swaggart were wielding in the United States. The idea that one could foment a religious revolution and also own a Rolls Royce and a house in Palm Springs, and have a glamorous wife, had an appeal to Abdullah that grew daily as the sun beat down on the construction trailer, and his wife feigned more headaches, and his father refused his requests to take another bride or two. So one day, oh what a day, Abdullah just up and quit.

Everyone in the Middle East knew the rest of the story. The anger of his father, who publicly threatened to disinherit him. The furor of the Saudi government, when the king learned that Abdullah was taking jihad so seriously as to upset the Bushes. The late-night flight on a bin-Salem corporate jet into exile in the barren mountains along the Afghan-Pakistan border. Had it been the right decision? Abdullah had his doubts. After all, things didn't exactly turn out so well for his buddy Osama, whose life had followed a similar, if more dramatic and widely publicized, arc. Now it was pretty much impossible to see a Rolls Royce or a Palm Springs mansion in his future. He was lucky to find a sure-footed camel and an untattered tent. As for the glamorous wife, well, at the age of forty-five, it looked as if sex was destined to be a bigger part of Abdullah's past than his future.

But here he was. He looked at his watch. He had an hour before Isha Salat, the last prayer of the night. Next to him was the leather pouch he'd rescued, which Ahmed had sent along with his chronicle of failure. Abdullah whispered a prayer of forgiveness to Allah and, withdrawing a key from his thawb, unlocked the pouch and removed a tightly wrapped package. Peeling away the paper, he saw copies of US Weekly, OK, Celebrity Digest, and Hustler, each several months old. With a half smile, he lay back on his damp mattress and prepared himself for a journey into the world he had left behind, a world he sorely missed.

CHAPTER 3

MONDAY, FEBRUARY 17
THE OVAL OFFICE
THE WHITE HOUSE WASHINGTON, DC

"Oh fuck!"

John Edsel watched helplessly as his semen shot onto the raw silk upholstery of the sofa that only last night had been featured in a PBS special about his wife's efforts to restore the White House to its former glory.

"What's the matter?" asked Bree, his aide of three months, whose last minute jerk of the head had caused this problem.

"Nothing. Nothing. Look, I'm sorry. But you have to go now. This is making me very nervous."

Bree pulled her thong back into place as she stood up. She buttoned her blouse and said, clearly angry: "Don't I at least get a wash cloth?"

The President of the United States gestured absently toward the private bathroom off his office.

"Hey, would you bring out a wash cloth for me?" he asked, thinking that a little moistening might remove the incriminating spot, which seemed to grow bigger and bigger by the minute.

Bree came out of the bathroom, her nose in the air and a fiery look in her eyes.

"Well, thanks for all the after glow," she snapped. "I thought I meant something to you. I guess I was wrong."

"You know how much I care about you, Bree," Edsel said, zipping his pants. But I'm going through a tough time right now. The first hundred days are almost up, and the damned press is already at my heels like a pack of rabid dogs. Jesus Christ, I'm supposed to be on my honeymoon."

"Your honeymoon?" Bree wrinkled her nose in confusion. "I thought you'd been married for, like, ages. I bet you've got kids my age."

Thanks for reminding me, Edsel thought.

"No, not that honeymoon. My honeymoon with the press, with Congress, with the public. They're supposed to cut me a little slack in the first hundred days. But look at this!"

Edsel spread the front page of The New York Times on his desk. There, above the fold, was an analysis by Adam Nagourney: "John Edsel: Did the Voters Buy a Lemon?" Edsel crushed the newspaper in his hand and tossed it into the trash. Under it was the Wall Street Journal, opened to the editorial page. "Who is John Edsel?" was the lead editorial. Edsel ripped that page apart and trashed it too.

Edsel escorted Bree out a door to his office and into a corridor where her presence would be noted only by Jack Northern, a Secret Service agent he trusted so thoroughly that he had named him to replace the Marine who traditionally stood outside the Oval Office door. He sat back at his desk and stared at the semen stain, which now seemed as big as the presidential seal woven into the center of the carpet. God, Betty was sure to see that. She'd hit up old Anabelle Ramsey for something like $10,000 just to reupholster that damned sofa. What a waste of money, money that could have gone to EdselPAC. Knowing Betty, she'd have the damned thing taken out and tested for DNA.

Edsel surveyed the stack of papers before him. Schedules,

briefings, proclamations. National Discount Auto Parts Dealers Month, National Ferret Day, National Pasteurized Cheese Manufacturers Day — boy, the money guys at the RNC had been busy! He had thirty minutes to sort through all of this before Jesus Ramirez, his Secretary of Labor, showed up for his monthly fifteen-minute meeting. The man was dumb as a box of rocks, and Edsel couldn't understand half of what he had to say. Hell, it had taken Edsel a few weeks to learn the man's name was pronounced "Hay Soos," and not "Jesus." Lockehart Jones had insisted Ramirez be appointed to cement relations with what he called "the Hispanic base." Lockehart knew his politics, but somehow Edsel felt strange appointing a man named Jesus, however you pronounced it, to a cabinet post. His poor mother, devout Southern Baptist that she was, probably was spinning in her Alabama grave at the thought of Jesus reporting to her son, instead of it being the other way around. For the first time all day, Edsel chuckled.

Lockehart should be the one to meet with Jesus and all of these other characters, Edsel thought. After all, in a way it was Lockehart who got him into all this, arguing that he should run for president when he'd been damned happy at the Governor's Mansion back in Montgomery. Edsel had never worked so hard. The campaign was as intense as the football training back at Mid-Alabama Tech, where he was the star quarterback. The actual job of president, though, was like those damned history and sociology courses he'd had to take in college. Edsel hadn't done well with them, and he knew the only reason he was able to graduate was because he was the best quarterback the Devils had ever had, and because the father of his high-school bride and their family manufacturing company were big contributors to the Mid-Atlantic Tech building fund.

The buzzer on his telephone sounded.

"Mr. President, Mr. Jones here to see you."

"Send him in," Edsel bellowed, sprawling back in his chair and putting his feet up. Damned if he was gonna let this job turn him into an office drone, although Betty would raise a racket if she saw his feet on this antique desk.

"Mr. President, good to see you, sir."

Lockehart Jones was tall, with a face like a young Mitt Romney and wearing a suit that looked as if it cost more than his annual salary as Special Advisor to the President. He moved across the vast expanse of presidential carpet with his hand outstretched, as though he were running for office himself.

"How ya doing, Locke?" said Edsel, ignoring the outstretched hand and not bothering to shift from his relaxed sprawl. "Listen, I got ole Jesus coming in here in a few minutes. So we gotta make it quick."

"Mr. President, please remember that it is pronounced 'hay soos.' Latinos will be offended if they think you are calling Mr. Ramirez 'Jesus. Anyway, sir, I took the liberty of postponing Secretary Ramirez's meeting until next month. There's an urgent matter I need to take up with you."

"Well, that's a relief. At least I can understand you when you talk. What's up Locke?"

"Mr. President, we finally have the results from last week's polling in, and we've got some problems. The big concern is voters see you as weak on terrorism and foreign policy. Also, you don't seem to be connecting with young people."

"Terrorism and foreign policy? Jesus Christ, Locke! I made that damned speech you wrote for me last week. Every single one of those geezers at the VFW Convention applauded. I even got a standing ovation — at least from the ones who could stand. The others were thumping their canes. And it's not like we've had any terrorist activity. I hear every morning about that terror alert, and it's been pink — I think it's pink, or is it orange? — every day since I've been elected."

"I know Mr. President. But the press has made a lot of noise about that pickup truck with all the fertilizer and chemicals that the police found in the parking lot of that Wal-Mart in Kansas. I know nothing happened. But suddenly people are worried again. I mean, if a Muslim terrorist could strike in the middle of Kansas, well then, no one's safe."

"Hell, how do they know it wasn't some damned farmer getting ready to fertilize a field? What makes them think it was a bomb? Okay, okay. So what do you want me to do about it Locke? I gotta go and make another damned speech? We gonna turn that light from pink to green or whatever? What do you want me to do?"

"Well, Mr. President, we think we know where Abdullah bin-Salem is hiding. We'd like authorization to kidnap him. This could be as big a deal as the assassination of Osama bin Laden."

"Abdullah bin-Salem? You're fucking kidding me! I mean, the whole damned world has been looking for that goober since bin Laden was killed and ain't been able to find him. Now you know where he is? Hell, Locke, let's just do it! Let's just damned well do it. We even could use that new Kudzu 990 helicopter my father-in-law is building if the damned Defense Department would just buy it."

"Thank you Mr. President. I knew you'd like this plan. Your administration will accomplish something the last two administrations failed at. You'll go down in the history books for this."

"And Locke, I want that son of a bitch brought here. I wanna see him. I wanna look him in the eye."

"Mr. President, I would advise against that. Our plan is to take him to Gitmo and intern him there. There could be legal ramifications if you bring him into the United States, and security issues, and …"

"Dammit Locke! You heard me. I want the bastard standing in front of me. I wanna be able to tell the American people I looked eye-to-eye with the asshole responsible for all this terror. I wanna be able to say I stared down that murderer. You hear me boy? There ain't gonna be any debate on this one, Locke. I want him here."

"Yessir, Mr. President. I hear you sir."

Lockehart Jones stood and gave the slightest bow as he made ready to leave. "Mr. President, there's one more thing. It's a minor problem, but I want to check with you."

"What is it Locke?"

"Well sir, regarding your problem in the polls with young people. There's an opportunity with London Comfort, the celebrity. She was arrested for speeding sir, in California, and it looks like she's going to be sentenced to prison for violating her probation. I wouldn't bring this up with you sir, except that her father, Ali Comfort, is one of your very biggest supporters. There's a chance, if you'd approve it, that we could convince the judge to order her to do community service instead of prison. It seems Ms. Comfort saw your wife's White House tour on television, and she's told her advisors that she would like to do community service at the White House, maybe as a tour guide. I know it's highly unusual sir, but it would really help us with the youth vote. It also would cement our relationship with Mr. Comfort and his fellow hotel owners."

"That's a great idea Locke! I guess that's why I have you on the payroll boy. Just make sure you let Betty know, will ya? She's in charge of the White House."

"Thank you sir. I'll take care of it."

Jones turned and began to move purposefully out of the President's office, when something caught his eye.

"Mr. President. Did you notice that spot on your sofa, sir? Is there a leak? Should I ask someone to take care of it?"

Edsel groaned and waved Jones out the door. The most powerful man in the world turned to his computer to Google solutions for upholstery stains.

CHAPTER 4

MONDAY, FEBRUARY 17
THE WEST WING, THE WHITE HOUSE
WASHINGTON, DC

Lockehart Jones walked down the West Wing hall to his office. Not sixty days in the White House, and John Edsel was already impossible. The man didn't read anything put in front of him. He couldn't pronounce the names of his own cabinet secretaries, much less those of the leaders of half the free world. Now that the campaign glad handing and speech reading were over, John Edsel was looking like the empty suit the Democrats said he was. To Jones, who had more than a casual interest in fashion, Edsel's wasn't even a good suit.

It was classic, Jones realized. The dumb straight guy in the top job, with the smart, yet closeted, gay guy making him look good. When the chairman of the Republican National Committee had first approached Jones for help in "packaging" Edsel, he was dubious and reluctant. Edsel's highest previous office had been as governor of Alabama, a state that distinguished itself by keeping Mississippi or Arkansas from ranking last on every list. As lieutenant governor, Edsel had inherited the governorship after the incumbent collapsed and died at his desk in a scandal Jones had helped hush up. The party chairman argued that at least Edsel wasn't Lydia Quinn, whose abrupt decision not to seek a second term as President had mystified everyone in the nation except for the people at Institute of Living, the private psychiatric hospital in Hartford, Connecticut, where party leaders had delivered her after a series of bizarre public statements that had made even Michelle Bachman, the GOP's newest reality TV star, sound sane. With Edsel, there were no pronouncements, no positions, no initiatives, and thus no record that the Democrats could make hay with. Edsel was a tabula rasa, the party chairman had said, trying to make a virtue of the fact that John Edsel hadn't had a single original idea or achieved anything of note in four years in public office. Within the party, Locke Jones, with the help of some expert polling and advertising, got most of the credit for turning John Edsel into a candidate who could secure the White House for the GOP for a second four years. John Edsel was the man who would finish paying off the US debt by selling off all the useless crap, including a few states, that had been accumulated over the years. With Edsel's inauguration, GOP majorities in the House and Senate, and seven justices sitting on the far right of the Supreme Court, the Democrats would have no more impact than those pesky mosquitoes Locke had to slap off during his campaign visits to Alabama.

Not that it had been easy. Even the guys at Halliburton, who had gotten assurances about Edsel from George W. Bush and Dick Cheney, who submitted a recommendation in writing from Leavenworth, were doubtful after they met the candidate. Jones had briefed Edsel thoroughly for that meeting, but it just hadn't stuck. Edsel confused Halliburton with Smithfield, their four p.m. donor call. His good ole boy jokes about "makin' bacon" didn't find a receptive audience. Then there were the problems with Edsel making three a.m. room service calls at hotels around the country, the goal being to score sex with chambermaids. Jones tried to put a stop to that by telling Edsel the story of

Dominique Strauss-Kahn. "You don't want your opponents of accusing you of acting like a Frenchman, Mr. President," he had said.

It was galling. Not only because Edsel was so stupid. He also was racist, and sexist, and homophobic. Jones knew Edsel's reputation for hitting on White House aides and interns. He knew he was carrying on with Bree Collard, a twenty-year-old whose D-cups were the only possible reason she scored a coveted White House job. Not that Jones could complain. He had used sex to curry favor on his own behalf, and for friends. It was a very, very friendly professor at Brown, who had served in several previous administrations, who had scored a White House post for Jones soon after his graduation. Jones himself had just helped Roberto Diaz, London Comfort's PR guy, whose private relations prowess was as amazing as his vaunted public relations skill. Still, Locke Jones wasn't the President of the United States.

What pissed off Jones was that Diaz could be himself, a real flamer, and still be a success in Hollywood public relations. Jones, in the White House, in the GOP, a few steps away from a redneck president, had to live in the closet. He couldn't even afford to be seen in one of those bars on "P" Street where gay congressional staffers and lower-level administrators in federal agencies would cluster, sometimes with one of the few "out" Congressmen in tow. It played hell with his love life. He didn't dare hire a hooker for fear he'd be blackmailed. That's where Roberto helped. He knew Jones' type — dark, ethnic — the opposite of the Boston super-WASP that was Lockehart Jones. When he met someone who he thought might measure up, Roberto would make the discreet introduction. Thanks to Roberto, Jones was working his way around the southern hemisphere, all without leaving the United States. In fact, he kept a world map on his bedroom wall, where colored pins identified the homelands of his sexual conquests. Latin America was a thicket of stickpins. Africa was pretty barren, except for a few pins in Cape Town and Rabat. Lately, Jones, with that drive to achieve that had made him a magna cum laude graduate of Brown, was focused intently on the Middle East. Israel was pricked with a dozen pins. There was one in Cairo. But the one Jones was most proud of was stuck right in the middle of Jeddah.

That was a new pin. Roberto had been in town to meet with some writers from the Washington Post a month ago, and he'd called Jones for a drink. When Jones showed up, Roberto was escorting a sexy guy, in his early thirties, with a dark complexion, a slight Southern accent, and a butt that couldn't be believed. "Locke, meet Abdul," Roberto said. "Abdul, meet Locke."

Roberto slipped out after fifteen minutes, leaving Abdul and Jones alone. A quick dinner at a nearby restaurant morphed into dessert at Jones' condo followed by breakfast the next morning — an early one, given Jones' seven a.m. start time at the White House. There was something about the strangeness of the other that excited Jones. Abdul, despite the complexion and the accent, was an Arab and Muslim, a turn-on for Jones, an Episcopalian who couldn't be bothered with practicing religion. He'd heard all those George Bush speeches about how Muslims were our friends, but Jones was turned on by sex with a guy who might have been just as happy killing him. There was something exotic and exciting in the pillow talk afterwards about Abdul's time in the Saudi army and his skill at slitting a sheep's throat to prepare for the Id-Ul-Fitra feast that ended Ramadan. Jones had to admit that Abdul's unavailability also made him alluring. He was an actor appearing in commercials overseas, and he wouldn't be back in the United States for another two weeks. To thank Roberto for the introduction, Jones had offered to use the power of the Oval Office to help Roberto's client, London Comfort, bunk in the White House for a few months instead of a Los Angeles jail.

Jones smiled to himself as he realized he was getting a hard on. Only the President should be walking around with a boner in John Edsel's White House. Quickest way to get rid of that was to place a call to the Secretary of Defense and tell her the plan to abduct Abdullah Bin-Salem was a go. People assumed Lockehart Jones was single because he worked so hard and was so devoted to his job. But they knew Secretary of Defense Cherry Samuels worked so hard and was so devoted to her job because she was single.

"Marsha, put me through to Secretary Samuels."

"Good afternoon Madame Secretary. Thanks for taking my call." Locke was unfailingly polite, even though he knew his position with the President, and the party, meant Cherry Samuels didn't have any choice but to take his call.

"Good to hear from you Locke. What's up today?"

"Hello, Madame Secretary. How is that helicopter evaluation going? Are Sikorsky and Mid-South Manufacturing still in the running? Curious whether there will be some Kudzu 990s joining the fleet, or whether we'll be sticking with Sikorsky's Black Hawk?"

"They're the two finalists, Locke. We should have a decision in two weeks. I'll keep you posted."

"Thank you ma'am. But the main reason I called is I've just talked with the President. We have authorization to proceed with Operation Ali Baba."

"Great, Locke. Wonderful news. I assume you'll tell the veep. I'll alert Admiral Roster."

"Ma'am, you should know there's a bit of a wrinkle in our plans. The President insists that we bring our prisoner here."

"Here? Oh fudge! Locke, you've gotta be kidding. I mean what if one of those judges grants a habeas petition? You can't even trust Clarence Thomas anymore. Since he had that stroke, he's been absolutely unpredictable. He's acting like he thinks he's Thurgood Marshall."

"I know Madame Secretary. I agree with you. But the President insists."

"Oh, fudge Locke! Oh, fudge."

CHAPTER 5

THURSDAY, FEBRUARY 20
CENTURY REGIONAL DETENTION FACILITY
LYNWOOD, CA

London, dressed in stained blue cotton pants and shirt and wearing rubber slippers, sat at a Formica-topped table in the visitor's lounge at the Century Regional Detention Facility. Across from her were the two most important people in her life, other than her father, and she didn't like what they were telling her.

She'd spent six nights in this horrible place, denied bail because she had violated probation and because she was deemed a "flight risk." Ralphie Soltis, her lawyer, was telling her she was sure to be found guilty if she demanded

a trial. That meant there was a good chance she

would go to jail for a few months. Her publicist, Roberto Diaz, nodded in agreement.

"A few months? It's so unfair! Roberto, can't you do something?"

If anyone could get her out of this, it was Roberto Diaz.

Luckily for her, he was gay as a goose. For one thing, London didn't have to worry about him hitting on her. For another, he was part of that Velvet Mafia the gossip columnists talk about. Her father and his friends always said the Jews ran the media. London knew better. The media was, like, totally queer! And Roberto was the queerest queer London had ever met. It seemed like he'd had sex with someone at every studio in Hollywood, on every entertainment news show, at every major newspaper, and every magazine. He must have been good, because when he called for favors, he and London got them.

"Baby, I wish I could," Roberto said. "But it looks like the judge who's going to hear your case isn't one of my friends, if you know what I mean. We've looked into it. He's married, Republican, as straight as a five-dollar bill. We do have an idea though. How would you like to work in the White House?"

"What white house?"

"The White House," Roberto said. "You know, the one where the President of the United States lives."

"I don't know," London said, very tentative. "It's in Washington? I've never been to Washington. I don't know anyone there."

"But baby," Roberto said. "You'd have your own room there. It's like a cool hotel. We think we could even get a TV deal out it."

"So what does this have to do with the judge and with me going to jail?" London asked.

Ralphie took this one.

"London, the judge is surely going to find you guilty. He's up for re-election soon. If he lets you loose, he's gonna get creamed. But we know he wants to be a federal judge. And, well, let's just say he'll have a crack at being a federal judge if he'll release you on what they call community service."

"You mean like picking up leaves and garbage in public, like Elton John?" London's frown said "no."

"We've got a classier idea for you," Roberto said. "That's where the White House comes in. You would be an intern or a tour guide at the White House! It's patriotic! It's noble! It's self-sacrifice! It's the new London Comfort — concerned for her country!"

"Intern? Tour guide? I don't know anything about the White House. What would I do? What would I say? Would I have to wear some geeky uniform?"

"No baby," Roberto said. "You'd dress like you always do. Well, maybe longer skirts, and maybe looser blouses. But pretty much the same. It would be like being a television host, except without the television cameras. Every day there would be a different audience, there to see London Comfort, and the White House. Whaddya say?"

"So how long would I have to do this? You're sure it would keep me out of jail?"

"Three months, tops," said Ralphie. "Monday through Friday, eight a.m. to five p.m., with an hour for lunch and a half hour break each morning and afternoon."

"Eight in the morning? Are you fucking kidding me?" London said. "Do you know how many lines of coke I'd have to do to be awake at eight in the morning? Ralphie, Roberto, get real."

"Baby, it's either that, or more of this," Roberto said, gesturing with open arms to the visitor's room, now full of enormous black and Latin women on London's side of the tables, and screaming babies and the tattooed gang members who fathered them on the other side.

"Okay. Okay." London relented. "I'll do it."

The alarm sounded to indicate the end of visiting hours. Roberto and Ralphie blew kisses across the table to London before turning to make their way through the throngs of people to the door. London stood for a moment, watching their backs recede, stunned by the enormity of what had happened to her and what was likely to continue happening. She joined the long line of women waiting for a pat down from one of the big prison matrons, who would make sure she wasn't smuggling a file or a gun or a lipstick back into her cell.

"Life is so unfair!" she complained to the young Latin woman standing in front of her, who rolled her eyes at hearing that from one of America's best known and wealthiest young women.

London couldn't believe the judge had denied her bail. He could have fixed one of those Martha Stewart ankle bracelets on her and let her go home, like some of the other girls in her cell when she first arrived. The prosecutor had argued that she was a flight risk. Like, where the hell was she going to fly? She wasn't about to pull a Roman Polanski and run away to Paris. The only thing French that she liked was the kissing and the fashion. The only time she had even flown out of the United States, other than for visits to resorts in Mexico and the Caribbean, which sort of belonged to the United States anyway, was against her will. That was twenty years ago, on September 13, 2001, and it had been a nightmare. She remembered all too well the last-minute call from her father's lawyer. They thought one of her mother's brothers had been involved in the Trade Center bombing, and they were trying to get them all out of the United States before other people learned about it.

London hadn't wanted to leave. After all, she told her mother, at the age of eight, with blonde hair and flawless gold skin, no one was going to mistake her for some Arab terrorist. Yes, her mother and father were Muslim, or at least they had been way back when they were growing up in Saudi Arabia. But now her mother and father were Bel Air through and through. And so was London. She didn't even really know what Muslim meant.

The lawyer had insisted though. She had thirty minutes to pack. Thirty minutes to pack! That was, like, so totally insane. Her nanny managed to throw only a few things into London's Vuitton by the time the car came for her and her mother. She'd been put in an economy seat in a chartered jet — even at that young age the first (and thankfully only) time in her life she'd flown in the back of an airplane. The meals were just awful. She'd already seen the in-flight movie. She was surrounded by strange people she was told were relatives. Some of the women wore those black shrouds that showed only their eyes and noses, an outfit her mother donned only just before the plane landed. The guys dressed normally, although they looked like dorks. It was strange the way they looked at her mother, like they were undressing her with their eyes and wanting to beat her up, all at the same time. Twenty-four hours later they landed in Saudi Arabia. Before she got off the plane, a woman came up and insisted London, because she looked more like she was thirteen than eight, also put on one of those black shrouds. It was awful, and it was made of muslin. Muslin, Muslim. There was forever a connection in London's mind. London's skin itched all the way to the hotel, where, once in her room, she finally was able to peel off that damned shroud and take a hot bath. Muslin was all wrong for delicate skin like hers.

A week or so later she was back in LA. No one had connected her parents or London with this Abdullah bin-Salem. When London asked her mother about him, she just rolled her eyes. "I have a dozen brothers, and a dozen sisters. You expect me to remember all of them?" she'd said.

After ten minutes of shuffling along in the line, it was London's turn to be patted down. She was surprised to recognize the woman cop who had arrested her.

"How you doing honey?" the woman asked, giving London one of the few smiles she had gotten in this place since she'd arrived.

"I don't know. Not so good," London said. "What are you doing here?"

"Got transferred. I wasn't with the Highway Patrol, you know. I was with the Sheriff's Department. Just got called out because they needed a woman to help bring you in. You're looking good honey. Hope you ain't letting this get you down."

"It is getting me down. It's not looking good for me. Uh, I'm sorry. I don't even know your name."

"My name is Kameela. You're London Comfort, the celebrity, right? Well, I gotta get this line moving. So I can't talk now. But I'll stop by a little later if you'd like."

"Sure," London said. "I mean, whatever. That would be nice."

London shuffled off to her cell. At least, because of her celebrity, she had one to herself. She'd heard horror stories about some of the other inmates. She'd had sex with other girls, and it had been fun, but only with guys involved too. The women in this prison — well, let's just say it was clear none of them had ever had a bikini wax. They looked like truck drivers.

The door to the cell clanged shut behind her. London was back in her little eight by ten room, with a single bed, a metal toilet bolted to the wall, and a metal sink with a metal mirror. The light was fluorescent. Never had she felt or looked so ugly. There was no TV, no radio, no iPod, no wireless Internet, no telephone. They told her they would order books for her, but London wasn't really the reading type. She was just so damned bored!

An hour must have passed when she heard someone quietly calling her name outside the cell door. It was Kameela.

CHAPTER 6

SUNDAY, FEBRUARY 23
CENTRAL AVENUE
SOUTH CENTRAL LOS ANGELES

It was hot, and it was long and sometimes hard to walk in. But in a place as dirty and depraved as her South Central LA neighborhood, Kameela Ishaad felt safe and secure in her burka. Now, standing in line at Honeys Kettle Fried Chicken, surrounded by men who otherwise would have been jiving to catch her eye, the burka let Kameela pretend she was in another place, a more beautiful place, a place where the air was scented with something other than burning chicken fat, and the land was covered with flowers and grass instead of junked cars, bone-thin dogs, and ramshackle houses. People who asked her about the burka assumed wearing it was a sacrifice she made to show her devotion to Allah. To Kameela, the burka was no sacrifice. It was one of the great joys of her faith. Her sacrifice came in not insisting on wearing it at work. She was sure she could have. After all, there were Sikhs in the department who wore their turbans. But Ahmed had asked her to keep a low profile on the job. That meant not wearing a burka, not following the ritual required for the daily prayers. Instead, when her wrist watch sounded the hour for the noon, afternoon, and sunset prayers, Kameela would perform her ablutions by briefly touching the clean, dry soil she carried to work in a Zip-Lock bag and wiping her hands and face. Then she stood for a moment and recited the Dhurh, 'Asr, and Maghrib prayers to herself. No one ever noticed. Kameela felt guilty about not following the prescribed ritual. But her imam had assured Kameela that Allah forgave her, indeed that Allah wanted her to hide her faith at work so that she would be able to undertake a very important mission. What that mission was, Kameela had yet to learn.

The young girl smiled as she passed the bag of fried chicken across the counter. Kameela took it and her super-sized cola and walked serenely past the young men on the street talking about the other women's butts. In her burka, Kameela was invisible to them.

The road from the A.M.E. Zion Church to Islam and the burka had started in Biddleville, the oldest black neighborhood in Charlotte, North Carolina, where Kameela never imagined an alternative to Christianity, as much a given in her life as sweet tea and biscuits. There was one Catholic kid in elementary school, who kept pretty much to herself and claimed she was a Christian too, although Kameela's friends weren't buying that. In high school, Kameela remembered hearing from classmates about the Jews, who had killed Jesus Christ and now were living in Myers Park, the fancy Charlotte neighborhood where Kameela's mother cleaned house. It was when she was eighteen, and visiting her aunt in New York City, that Kameela first became aware of women in head-to-toe black gowns who glided like swans through the filthy and chaotic streets of Harlem, women they called Muslim.

Kameela was just getting acquainted with New York City's club scene and falling into a world of sex, drugs, and music that reminded her nightly that she wasn't back in North Carolina. She wondered why a woman would want to hide herself from all that.

"Why are they dressed like that?" she'd asked a friend one

day, as they encountered three swans moving through the jostling Saturday sidewalk crowds outside a store where Kameela had spent a week's housecleaning wages on a red silk thong and bra.

Shantay rolled her eyes.

"They say it's religion. I say it's because they can't get laid, and they just decided to quit trying. But girl, it's good news for us. Less competition on the street!"

Kameela laughed then, but after six months in New York, much as she liked the attention of the men she was into, she found herself increasingly angry about the lewd comments from strangers about the size of her butt and the loud speculation about what she'd be like in bed. Men would grab at her on the sidewalk, in the clubs — always the men she didn't want to be touching her. She'd bought a small penknife, and twice she'd drawn blood when a man got too close. The black swans, as Kameela came to know them, swam through the obscene stream unnoticed, unassaulted, and seemingly unperturbed.

Three years and two crazy lovers later, Kameela had remembered those black swans as she sat in front of a sheriff's deputy on Newton Street in South Central LA, a continent away, and stared at color photos of the bloody face of Junious Peeples. The Kameela who looked at those photos had turned into one tough bitch, able to give as well as she got. She always carried a thin and sharp blade that she had used more than once to slice up a persistent nigga. The most recent had been Peebles, the Compton drug king, whose bloody but smirking face was staring up at Kameela in a photo on the gray linoleum surface of the deputy's desk. It was, Kameela knew, Peebles' word against hers. The deputy, feigning concern about Kameela, said she understood what Kameela had done, that she probably would have done the same thing if someone had tried to rape her. She'd make sure Kameela got treated right if she explained what happened. But Kameela wasn't confessing. She seen enough cop shows to know this empathy wasn't real.

"No ma'am, I don't know him."

"No ma'am, that man, he didn't touch me."

"No ma'am, I ain't never cut no one."

"No ma'am, I don't own a knife, 'cept for one for butter."

Three hours later, Kameela was released without being charged. She swaggered out of the station, wearing the lascivious but tough smile that had become her public mask. She stepped out of the taxi in front of her apartment building, smirking at the gangstas on the steps across the street as they called out "yo bitch, gimme some of that." When she got to the fourth floor, she unlocked the door to her apartment, threw off her clothes, and collapsed. Kameela screamed, biting into her pillow to mask the noise, although it was unlikely a scream in her building would attract any serious attention. She screamed and she cried, trying with all her might to empty her body, empty her mind, empty her soul, of every last bit of the Kameela she had become. In the journey from Biddleville to Harlem to Los Angeles, the little girl whose shy smile could charm the sternest elementary school teacher, whose giggle could melt her distant mother's oft-frozen heart, had hardened and tempered until now she was as cold, sharp, and dangerous as the knife she'd carefully hidden in the oven when the sheriff's deputy knocked on her front door. Kameela didn't know what had happened. Now, however, she knew what to do about it.

The next morning Kameela got out of bed, walked into the bathroom, showered, and threw the lipsticks, the rouge, the perfume, the hair straightener, into the trash. Back in her bedroom, she tore through her closet, tossing into a garbage bag the tight-ass pants, the thongs, the porn star blouses. She slipped a white shift over her head, climbed down the stairs, and walked through the front door of the building to the street, the usual gang of bruthers apparently rendered speechless by the uncharacteristic modesty and tranquility that she projected. Twenty minutes in a taxi and Kameela found herself at the door of the Muslim Women's Association and on the front steps of a whole new life.

CHAPTER 7

FRIDAY, FEBRUARY 28
THE WEST WING, THE WHITE HOUSE
WASHINGTON, DC

There were days when Lockehart Jones wondered why he held this thankless job. This was one of them. It had started with The New York Times story about London Comfort's appearance the day before on the Barry Show, something Jones hadn't been consulted on. Now Jones sat in the office of the very angry press secretary watching the video of an obviously amused Barack Obama — the new Oprah they called him — quizzing America's most famous know-nothing celebrity about her upcoming gig at the White House. The woman's stupidity was truly amazing. Jones thought she might even rival John Edsel when it came to ignorance about the world they lived in.

What would London do if she ran the White House, Obama asked?

"Well, you know, I haven't been there yet?" she said, her voice tilting the end of the statement into a question in that annoying Valley Girl way. "But I've seen pictures. I mean, it kinda needs some color. And the swimming pool? I mean, it's inside! How can you tan if the swimming pool is inside? What if you want to give a pool party?"

Had London ever gotten involved in politics? Had she ever voted?

"I was one of the judges who voted on America's Top Model. I was one of the judges on So You Think You Can Dance."

Had London ever been outside of the United States? Were there countries or cities outside the U.S. that she'd like to see?

"I've been to Cancun! I know it's in South America, because I had to have a passport? I went to the Eiffel Tower, the one in Las Vegas. I mean, when you live in LA, you sort of have everything? So I can't think of a city I want to see!"

With each question, Obama flashed his famous grin. With each answer, Jones groaned. Americans were famously suspicious of intellectuals — a trait the GOP had used to its advantage for the past twenty years. Jones didn't believe that meant voters admired outright stupidity in their leaders (although there was a lot of pushback on that point from party operatives). Jones feared President Edsel already was walking the narrow line between dumb and "man of the people" with his proud declaration during the campaign that he'd never set foot out of the United States and couldn't be bothered to learn the names of the countries of Europe. It had been awkward when Edsel met the president of Georgia, the one who flew in from Tbilisi, and then proclaimed his deep affection for Atlanta and the Falcons while Mikheil Saakashvili, who apparently didn't understand English, smiled benignly. Now, as that fifteen-minute interview with London Comfort drew to a close, Jones worried that a PR coup intended to build support for Edsel among young people might turn into a disaster. And it would be his disaster, the press secretary reminded him. Jones flipped to The New York Times editorial page, where the top headline read "Dumb and Dumber?"

Jones knew the day would only get worse — Betty Edsel wanted to talk to him about what he planned to do with London Comfort. He scurried to the First Lady's East Wing office. For the first time since arriving at the White House in January, Jones thought his job might be on the line. He wasn't sure he cared.

He arrived promptly at ten a.m. Lydia Crinkle, Betty Edsel's secretary, pointed to a seat in the anteroom and told him the First Lady would see him when she was free. Jones, the man everyone knew as first among equals on President Edsel's staff, wasn't accustomed to this sort of treatment. There wasn't a Cabinet member who wouldn't drop whatever he or she was doing when Lockehart Jones came calling. Jones was beginning to get a deeper sense of who wore the pants in the Edsel family.

He knew Betty Edsel was richer than her husband — it was her family money that had bankrolled Edsel's first campaign for Lieutenant Governor of Alabama. He also knew she was smarter. On those rare occasions when Jones was with both the President and the First Lady, he always saw a bemused smile on her face while the President spoke, mangling the English language like a tractor rolling through kudzu. In some ways, Jones thought, this woman might be another Laura Bush. In another sense, she might be another Hillary Clinton. Had she heard the rumors about the President's frisky behavior with young female interns and assistants?

After a twenty-minute wait, Crinkle, with a smile that said she knew she had put Jones in his place, announced that the First Lady would see him. Jones stepped into a room that was the antithesis of the Oval Office. Where the President's formal office spoke of power and formality, the First Lady's office was nothing so much as a comfortable living room, dominated by a pair of white couches and a large round mahogany table at which Betty Edsel sat.

"Mr. Jones. Please have a seat," Mrs. Edsel said. "And please explain to me what the hell is going on."

Lockehart Jones, for the first time in his White House tour of duty, found himself stammering as he tried to explain London Comfort to the First Lady. He told her about the youth vote issue and the importance of Ali Comfort's contributions to EdselPAC. Betty Edsel just looked and listened, not asking a single question. Jones felt like he was sinking deeper and deeper into the hole he'd dug with London Comfort. He noticed the faintest flicker of a smile on her face. The First Lady was enjoying this.

"Well," she said, when Jones's explanations had petered out, "you've handed us a lemon. Now your job is to make lemonade. So I would like Miss Comfort to report directly to you. There's a lot we're going to have to teach this young lady, starting with manners and how to dress. While I question your judgment in this matter, I don't question your sense of style. We're also going to have to teach her about the White House — its history — before we can ask her to be a guide. From what I've seen on television, history isn't one of her strong suits."

At that, Betty Edsel stood, sending Locke Jones a clear signal that their meeting was over. He hustled back to the West Wing for a meeting with the Secretary of Defense. From Hollywood celebrity to Middle Eastern terrorism. Before the day was out, he had to put the capture of Abdullah bin-Salem in motion.

CHAPTER 8

FRIDAY, FEBRUARY 28
REAGAN NATIONAL AIRPORT
WASHINGTON, DC

London dreaded the idea of living in Washington, DC, almost as much as she'd dreaded her time at the Central Regional Detention Facility in Los Angeles. So there was something reassuring, comforting, about the crowd of photographers and reporters that confronted her as she walked through Washington National Airport on this sunny Friday morning, followed by two porters pushing carts stacked high with her Vuitton luggage. Roberto Diaz was on her left, shouting out the standard "No comment, there will be no comment." On her right was Kameela Ishaad, the tough prison guard London had hired as a bodyguard. The woman London had seen as a brutal beast the night of her arrest had morphed into the sort of friend London had heard existed but never known. Kameela wasn't impressed by London's celebrity. She didn't want to hang out with London's friends. She'd never heard of the reality TV show that brought London to the world's attention. Yet she had stopped by

London's cell every day at Central to talk and offer, in a voice so soft London sometimes strained to hear her, advice on surviving the insanity of a Los Angeles County jail. London's father, mightily distressed by her arrest, had insisted that his daughter finally hire a bodyguard who also would serve as her driver. For London, the choice was obvious. Only one person at South Central had shown her any kindness; she wanted to return the favor. London's father wasn't happy to see that Kameela wore a burka in her new job. London, on the other hand, thought it was kind of cool. She'd let her father have his way by hiring a bodyguard. She wouldn't let him decide who she'd hire, or what Kameela would wear.

Outside the airport, the sidewalk was clotted with even more photographers. Kameela, taking advantage of her size, barreled through them, creating a path for London and Diaz and the porters to the two limos — one for the people, one for the luggage — waiting at the curb.

"Maybe this town won't be so boring after all," London said, settling into her seat as the cameras continued to flash.

"Now London, you're going to have to be careful," Diaz said. "Everyone is going to be watching you. If you make one mistake, you could end up back in jail. No nightlife, no partying, no playing around. You have to be at the White House at eight each morning."

"Oh my God!" London wailed. "I thought you were kidding before. Eight in the morning? Really? I don't go to sleep most nights until two or three. I'm going to need some pills Roberto. I don't know how I can survive three months of this."

"Well, it could have been worse. At least you'll be staying at a hotel instead of the White House, which is a damned stuffy place. We have you booked into the Hay-Adams, right across the street from where you'll be working. You'll be in the Federal Suite, and Kameela will be right next door. A week from now you're having dinner with the President and his wife, Betty. A good friend of mine will be there too. He's a senior advisor to the President, and he'll be your mentor, your guide. His name is Locke Jones. So if you have any questions, he's the man to ask."

"I have to have dinner with them?" London pouted. "I mean, how old are they? They're like as old as my grandparents, right?"

"Well, as far as I know London, your grandparents are dead," Diaz said. "So they're not that old. I guess the President is about sixty, and his wife is a little younger. You'll like Locke Jones though. He's a fun guy. Just make sure you listen to him. He's the guy who's going to get your through all this. Who knows, maybe there's a TV show in it after it's over?"

London smiled.

The Federal Suite was stuffy for London's tastes, with formal furniture in the living room, although it did have a small balcony that offered a view of the White House. After the porters delivered London's luggage, and a hotel maid put everything away, London sank onto the sofa and poured herself a gin and tonic. She took a long sip and then noticed Kameela kneeling in the corner on a small rug and mumbling words London didn't understand.

"Kameela, are you all right?" London was a bit alarmed at this strange behavior.

In a manner of seconds, Kameela was standing again, facing London.

"Yes ma'am. I was praying."

"First, Kameela, I told you not to call me ma'am. That makes me feel so old! Call me London. I've heard of praying before dinner, and praying when you go to bed. But praying at .... what?" London checked her watch. "One-twenty five in the afternoon?"

London patted the seat on the couch next to her, indicating that Kameela should take a seat. As Kameela settled on the sofa, she removed the veil that covered the lower half of her face and pushed back her head covering, revealing her tight brown curls. She knew it was time to come out of the closet if she was going to spend three months in such close quarters with London. It was time to own her religion.

"I am a Muslim, ma'am," Kameela said. London's glare startled Kameela, who realized that her revelation had just cost her her job. Then Kameela remembered what London had just told her. "I'm sorry. I am a Muslim, London."

"That's, like, so cool," London gushed. "I mean, I sort of knew that when I saw your outfit. But I thought you were from North Carolina. How did you become a Muslim from there?"

While London sipped her drink, Kameela began the story of her long journey from North Carolina to Los Angeles, from Southern innocence to gang violence, and the redemption and relief she found in her new faith. London, who constantly checked her cell phone during any other conversation, this time gave Kameela her undivided attention, interjecting only an occasional question.

"I'm so proud of you for becoming who you really want to be," London told Kameela. "I'm trying to figure that out for myself. Some day I'll have to tell you how I became London Comfort. "

"London, it is not my intention to make you a Muslim. But I want to give you a copy of the Koran. I am happy to discuss this life with you. You might find it comforting," Kameela said.

London opened the Koran that Kameela handed her. "This Koran! It looks so difficult. Is there a Koran for dummies? Or maybe a video about it?"

London laughed. She reached over and hugged Kameela, who returned the embrace.

CHAPTER 9

FRIDAY, FEBRUARY 28
THE PENTAGON
WASHINGTON, DC

Lockehart Jones insisted on meeting personally with the Navy Seals tasked with capturing Abdullah bin-Salem. Cherry Samuels and Admiral Roster, the Navy secretary, were mightily annoyed at this violation of Defense Department procedure.

"Mr. Jones, having you meet directly with members of our Special Operations Force contradicts our chain of command," said Roster, a thirty-year veteran rumored to be next in line to chair the Joint Chiefs of Staff.

"I'm sorry Admiral Roster. This isn't my decision. The President himself asked me to hold this meeting. He would be doing it if his schedule allowed. He wants to make sure that every one of these men knows that Abdullah bin-Salem is to be brought back alive. 'Alive and kicking.' Those were President Edsel's exact words."

"I want to go on record, Mr. Jones, in opposition to this decision to bring bin Salem back to Washington. There are so many things that could go wrong. If someone outside the highest levels of the chain of command finds out, we might get pressured by judges to release him for prosecution in a civilian court. This can't be about the President's ego, Mr. Jones. This has to be about the security of the United States."

Cherry Samuels winced at Roster's comments, but she didn't speak up to disagree. Jones agreed with him. This was another case where John Edsel was putting ego ahead of common sense.

"I understand your concerns sir," Jones said. "To prevent that, the President has agreed we need to keep this operation as secret as possible. Mrs. Samuels and yourself, the CIA Director. That's all. Oh, Jack Northern, who heads the President's Secret Service team."

Jones had suggested adding Northern to the bin-Salem team, and he was happy that he said yes. Northern was one of the few White House staffers Jones felt he could trust. One of the few who was rational and smart and modest. One of the few, given his access to the President, who knew what Edsel was like and worried with Jones about the President's sexual peccadilloes. Northern had agreed with him that bringing bin-Salem to Washington was a crazy idea. Northern also agreed that President Edsel, when he had his mind set, wasn't easily dissuaded. Jones had to admit that he liked that Northern also was easy on the eyes. At six-two, lean, with a chiseled face, blue eyes, a blond buzz cut, and a ready smile that he clearly struggled to suppress so he could look "official," Northern was a hottie. It was clear, however, that he didn't play on Jones' team. Northern had a law degree from Princeton, and Jones wondered why someone with such a credential would have taken a job like this.

Samuels and Roster were more than a bit surprised when Jones insisted that no one tell the Vice President or the Secretary of State about this mission. The Secretary of State's name rarely surfaced when Jones talked with the President. Both Edsel and Lockehart distrusted that SOB with a Harvard degree, who was named to the job because of the lobbying by Halliburton and Exxon, on whose boards he sat, and because, well, because they needed someone in the Edsel White House who knew where all those countries were and now to pronounce their names.

The Vice President? Edsel liked him. "That man serves up a mean burger," the President said, more than once. But to Lockehart, an African-America Tea Party conservative, albeit one whose burger chain gave him business chops, was someone to be cautious about. Lockehart thought Jesse Grant, given his race, was as unlikely a real conservative Republican as Lockehart was. The man had even been a Democrat when he first ran, unsuccessfully, for the Mississippi legislature. Add to that Grant's mysterious biography, or lack of one. No one had been able to definitively construct his family tree. He had no previous political experience. Grant, who constantly bragged about his impoverished upbringing in rural Mississippi, explained away his lack of a birth certificate by saying that the white folks didn't bother to record the births of poor blacks where he grew up. His conservative political stance insulated him from any of the suspicions that had haunted Barack Obama. Even now, six years after Obama had resigned his Presidency to take a job with Oprah Winfrey as host of the Barry Show, the nuttiest right-wingers continued to write the White House and insist that the man be deported. Locke Jones wondered if they shouldn't focus their suspicion on Grant. He wasn't convinced the Vice President was all he claimed to be.

A knock on the door provided a welcome interruption to the awkward conversation in Samuels' office. The door opened and the twenty-four young men, dressed in their blue-gray pixilated uniforms and black boots, crowded inside, saluting the admiral and then standing at ease. Jones delivered the President's message. In unison, the men responded: "Yes sir." Then Jones stood to follow them out of the office and tried to remind himself, as those incredibly masculine and fit young men marched down the hall, that he was at work and might trip and fall if he didn't look where he was going. Jones checked his cell phone. Seven o'clock. Friday night. He'd been at it for twelve hours. Time to drag himself out of the White House and back to what little life he had on the outside — maybe some randy Internet chat! He knew that was pathetic. But Lockehart Jones was a careful man. He would never be caught tapping his toes in an airport toilet stall. And Saturday? There was an eight a.m. meeting with London Comfort. His was a job that never ended. The good news was Jack Northern would be joining them. Jones heard a buzz, looked at his cell phone, and broke into a smile. Abdul was in town, looking for someone to join him for a Saturday night dinner, and a Sunday morning breakfast. "Cool," Jones texted back. "I'll put fresh sheets on the bed :))."

CHAPTER 10

FRIDAY, FEBRUARY 28
THE OVAL OFFICE, THE WHITE HOUSE
WASHINGTON, DC

The door to the Oval Office opened.

"It's time!" Susan Sweetzer, John Edsel's secretary, tapped the face of her watch and pointed up.

John Edsel groaned. Seven o'clock. Time to head upstairs for dinner with the wife. There wasn't much to look forward to when it came to dinner with Betty, not least because she had put him on a diet. Edsel knew that damned Locke Jones was behind that. "Look what happened to Chris Christie," Betty said whenever Edsel complained that fried chicken and mac and cheese were no longer on the menu. "Look what happened to Chris Christie," Jones would say when Edsel attempted to order an afternoon dessert from the White House kitchen. Christie getting stuck behind the wheel of his car, and having to have someone cut the steering wheel loose to get him out, had been fodder for the late night talk show hosts for weeks. Some thought the ridiculous situation was responsible for Christie's failure to win the New Jersey race for the U.S Senate. The American public was notoriously fat, but it didn't want its leaders to be. Hypocrites!

Solid food wasn't the only thing missing at the Edsel's dining table. There was little real conversation. At dinner, Betty always wanted to discuss international stuff, the economy. John Edsel felt like he was back at Pine Forest High School, taking an exam. After they finished dinner, they'd go to separate rooms to watch TV. He couldn't sit through one of those damned PBS leftist liberal specials where everyone spoke with a British accent. She rolled her eyes when he tuned into those reality TV shows ("White House Wife Swap!" — Edsel thought that would be a helluva idea for a show. Too bad Carla Bruni's husband, the one with the name Edsel couldn't pronounce, wasn't the president of France any more.) Betty usually was first to bed. Later Edsel would roll in beside his sleeping wife. Rarely did he wake her, or she wake him, for the sort of sex they'd had in the early years of their marriage.

Edsel had met Betty in homeroom during his freshman year of high school. At first, she hadn't made much of an impression. She was smart and quiet. She was always the first one to raise her hand when the teacher asked a question, which Edsel liked because it reduced the chance the teacher would ask him. She was good looking, in a country club sort of way. But sexy wasn't the first word that came to mind when one thought about Betty Evans.

By the time Edsel began his junior year at Pine Forest High School, he was far and away the biggest man on campus. Being quarterback of the Pine Forest Rebels assured that. The girls were all over him. He also was a party boy. Every Friday and Saturday night he and his buds hung out at the Burger Boy drive in, less for the burgers than the constant circling of girls, giggling from their car windows, and the beer and booze that the boys kept hidden in an ice chest under a blanket in the back seat. Life was like that well into the Fall of his junior year. Then two things conspired to convince Edsel Jones to settle down. First was that visit from Junebug Sandy's father just before Halloween. Big as

Edsel was, at six-feet-two and two hundred and twenty-five pounds, he was frightened as he sat across the kitchen table and listened to Roscoe Sandy proclaim that John Edsel had gotten fourteen-year-old Junebug pregnant. Edsel's mother had gasped and clapped her hand to her mouth and cried. Edsel's father, a taciturn mechanic, just groaned. Second was the meeting with the Pine Forest guidance counselor, who informed Edsel and his parents that college wasn't likely, given Edsel's poor grades. Again, Edsel's mother had gasped, clapped her hand to her mouth, and cried. Again Edsel's father had groaned. Neither of them had graduated from high school, much less college. They both had assumed that Edsel's athletic prowess might translate into a college scholarship for their only child.

"Boy, there's a way out," Roscoe Sandy told the Edsel family during their kitchen confrontation. "You know what it says in Colossians 3:13, right?"

Edsel and his parents nodded "no."

"Bear with each other and forgive whatever grievances you may have against one another," Sandy said, quoting the Bible. "Forgive as the Lord forgave you.

"Young man, I'm going to forgive you, on one condition. I want you to start going to church. If you start attending Sandy Hill Baptist Church — for services and Sunday School — I ain't going to call the police on you. I'm hoping that will inspire you to accept Jesus Christ as your savior."

Edsel nodded his head in the affirmative and looked at his parents, whose faces were washed with relief.

"What about the baby, sir?" he asked.

"That's a problem son. I'm going have to have Junebug visit her aunt in Gulfport to take care of that. You understand I ain't okay with taking a human life. A fetus is a human life. On the other hand, I can't accept having my daughter give birth to the spawn of your evil seed. I am going to pray to the Lord for forgiveness."

Edsel started attending Sandy Hill Baptist Church the following Sunday. The services put a crimp in his social life, not least because a nine a.m. youth group met before the eleven a.m.

church service each Sunday. That made partying until four a.m. out of the question. At the youth group meetings, where he steered clear of Junebug Sandy, John Edsel got to know Betty Evans, migrating over several months from the back row to the front row of the meeting, where Betty always sat. She was the only good-looking girl in the room, so that eventual migration was a given. Once he got to know her, Edsel discovered that Betty Evans wasn't as shy and retiring as he'd thought. The trashy girls at Pine Forest had been good at hinting when they wanted sex. Betty Evans was upfront in a different way. She didn't so much ask but order Edsel to meet her for dinner after a church service for what turned out to be their first date. Edsel still remembered the chicken fried steak he'd ordered that night, and the padded blue cushions in the booth where they sat, which were amazing like those of his desk chair in the Oval Office. Their conversation was an even more vivid memory.

"You've got quite a reputation," Betty had said as soon as the waitress had waddled away to the kitchen with their order.

Edsel hadn't been sure where that was going. He already was thrown off guard by the idea that a girl had asked him on a date, instead of the other way around.

"Thanks," he said. "It kind of comes with being the quarterback."

"So being the quarterback means you sleep with half the girls in the junior class? Is that a requirement, like keeping at least a B minus average?"

Betty smiled. Edsel was speechless.

"Is there a drinking requirement too? How much Jack and Coke does a guy have to drink on a Saturday night to stay on this team? I guess there's a PBR requirement too?"

"I, uh. I don't know what you're getting at."

"John, you are one sweet guy. I never picked up on that watching you on the field during the football games. I never noticed it seeing you in the hallway at high school, with all those flirty girls around you, winking and grinning, and those other guys high-fiving you. But it started seeping out when you first sat next to me at Sandy Hill. It's like there's some secret John Edsel all bottled up inside, and you don't think the guys and girls at Pine Forest are going to like the taste of that. So you keep a lid on it. I'm feeling it though John. I like the flavor."

This girl was scaring the hell out of him. But before that dinner was over, John Edsel also realized he was falling in love. His mother, distant and fragile, had never demanded anything of him. His father? Well, when he wasn't working, his father was drinking, his grease-encrusted hands holding one beer bottle after another until he fell asleep each night in front of the TV. For the first time in his life, John Edsel had met someone who was curious about him. Someone who asked for what she wanted and held him accountable. Someone who cared about him. He decided he needed to find answers to the questions she asked.

On May 19, 1978, the day after high school graduation and almost nineteen months after that first dinner in the Full Moon Diner, John Edsel and Betty Evans walked into the office of the justice of the peace in nearby Spoonerville to be proclaimed man and wife. To say that the Pine Forest High School student body, and for that matter the faculty, was shocked at the news of the marriage would have been an understatement. Edsel heard from his male friends that Julie Buncomb and Sally Sandifer had cried on one another's shoulders when they heard the news. Both had been among Edsel's earliest sexual conquests. Edsel's parents were stunned as well when they got the call from the justice of the peace's office. His mother and father were speechless, although that wasn't very revealing, given that speechless was pretty much their usual state of being. Betty Evan's parents, however, were anything but speechless when John and Betty called them. Jackson Evans, his voice trembling in an earthquake of anger, demanded that John and Betty drive immediately to his house to explain themselves.

"I wanna know why the hell I shouldn't get this damned marriage annulled?" Evans thundered at Edsel, when they met an hour after the marriage ceremony, in the tastefully furnished living room of the Evans mansion at the outskirts of town. "I wanna know why I shouldn't have your sorry ass kicked from here to hell and gone? I wanna know if you've been having sex with my daughter!"

Jackson Evans made the intimidating Roscoe Sandy look like a pansy. Evans wasn't a big man, the way Sandy was. In fact, John Edsel dwarfed his new father-in-law, who stood maybe five foot six and couldn't have weighed more than one hundred fifty pounds. But Evans's demeanor gave him a heft and stature that would have scared the NFL's biggest linebacker. The founder and president of Deep-South Manufacturing, the area's biggest employer, and one of Alabama's wealthiest men, Evans knew what power was and how to exert it.

The only question Edsel knew he could answer was the one about sex. To his amazement, he hadn't yet slept with Betty, not that he hadn't tried. She had told him there would be no sex until there was a ring on her finger. Edsel knew it said something about his attraction to Betty Evans that he hadn't just walked away. No other girl at Pine Forest High School had held out past the third date. Betty Evans had held John Edsel at bay for almost two years.

"No sir," Edsel told Evans. "We haven't had sex sir. We haven't had our honeymoon yet. We just got married."

Evans glared at Edsel. Slowly the hard and angry look softened.

"You know what boy? I think I believe you," Evans said.

"Sir, I love your daughter. She loves me," Edsel said. "We talked about having a big wedding, about all the invitations, and the planning, and the long engagement. But sir, we realized we loved each other. That was all that mattered. So we just decided to do it."

It took only a few weeks for Evans to yield. He had grown to like Edsel while he and Betty were dating. He was impressed that Edsel and his daughter had forged their relationship at Sandy Springs Baptist. A football fan, he admired Edsel's prowess as a quarterback. What worried him was the boy's future. Evans knew, however, that his checkbook could take care of that. He called a couple of friends on the Mid-Alabama Tech board. Yes, it was late to be admitting a freshman student for the upcoming semester. Yes, it was late to be trying out someone for the Mid-Alabama Devils. Yes, a check for two hundred fifty thousand dollars to begin construction on the hall that would house the Jackson Evans Institute of Biblical Studies would be much appreciated.

The phone rang. It was Betty, clearly annoyed. Time to put the past behind him and move into the future, whose immediate prospect was a near-vegetarian meal.

"Yes ma'am. I'm sorry. Got stuck here in the office dealing with one of those damned A-rab things. I'll be right up for dinner."

Edsel threw his feet off the desk and onto the floor, struggled into his suit jacket, and walked toward the door. Tonight it was some sort of fancy salad with soup. Hardly enough to sate the appetite of a man like him. Speaking of sating appetites, there was still that damned semen stain on the sofa. Betsy, who wasn't in the Oval Office very often, hadn't yet noticed it. But Edsel realized he was pushing his luck. Eventually she would, and she'd ask about it, and she wouldn't believe him, no matter how good a story he told. There'd be hell to pay. Edsel sighed and picked up the phone to call Jack Northern, his favorite Secret Service agent and the only man he'd trust with an assignment this delicate. Northern would get someone to clean that sofa pronto. Edsel stared at the stain. He had so many appetites, and so few ways in this job, in this marriage, of satisfying them.

Henry E. Scott

CHAPTER 11

FRIDAY, FEBRUARY 28
FAMILY RESIDENCE DINING ROOM
THE WHITE HOUSE, WASHINGTON, DC

It was aggravating. A waiter kept opening the door to peak into the dining room and see if the President had arrived. Betty Edsel knew the consommé was getting cold. She hoped the chef hadn't put together the salad — tonight it was flank steak with frisée and charred pepper salsa. The hot steak was supposed to wilt the frisée slightly. Fifteen minutes would make it all a mess.

At seven sixteen John Edsel walked into the dining room, stopping by Betty's chair to give what seemed to her to be a perfunctory kiss.

"How was your day, darling?" she asked.

"Another day, another dollar," he replied, a rote response that she heard all too often from him. It was if he were telling her that his day was none of her business. As usual, he didn't ask about her day.

Most of the time when the meal started like this, Betty got angry, and they settled into a cold silence until the meal was over.

Tonight she thought she'd try a different tack.

"John, I was going through some photos this afternoon, looking for a picture of my mama. I found a couple of that sweet little house we moved into just off the Mid-Alabama campus. You remember it, don't you?"

"Remember it? How could I forget it?" John Edsel put down his soupspoon and looked up at Betty and smiled. "You remember those rose bushes in the front yard? The ones that died when I gave them too much fertilizer?"

Betty laughed.

"And that little bedroom. You put all that fancy flower wallpaper up. Made me think I was sleeping in the girls' dorm. Not that I ever did. I promise you that!"

"That was a nice bedroom, wasn't it? There are days when I miss it, fancy as the bedroom here is. It was a small bed — couldn't have been more than a double. We were closer then, John, closer in so many ways."

Edsel pursed his lips and looked down at the bowl in front of him. Betty had tried to go there before. He wasn't good at this sort of conversation.

Betty realized that once again she'd wandered down a path that was headed nowhere. She changed direction.

"Well, I hope you like the salad. It's got some beef in it. After all, I don't want you to think I'm trying to turn you into a vegetarian. That wouldn't play well with your political base." She smiled.

Just then a waiter stepped forward to spirit away their soup bowls while another delivered the salads. Betty hated the way her attempts at intimate conversation in this house, rare as they were, got interrupted by waiters and maids and Secret Service agents and other servants. John found such interruptions a relief.

Once the table was cleared, John got up and headed to the TV room. There was a basketball game on, and he wasn't going to miss it. He settled onto the couch and lit a cigar — this was one federal building where smoking wasn't banned. Betty moved to a sitting room where the butler had already tuned the television to PBS and a rerun of one of her favorite British sitcoms. A waiter brought her a cup of tea.

Betty had trouble paying attention to what was on the screen. All she could think about was the man in the other room, half of what their college friends had idolized as the perfect couple. He was seen as the big, strong, and handsome one. Her girlfriends made her blush when they described her as beautiful and smart and composed. To their friends, they were the exemplars of married life.

For sure, there were some early problems. Not being able to have children was one of them. Not that they didn't try. But sex guided by doctors, with the goal being insemination of an egg instead of orgasmic pleasure, depressed Betty. She imagined it depressed Edsel too, although as their marriage grew older they talked less and less about intimate issues. These days they had sex maybe once a month, if that, and Betty wondered if Edsel found her attractive any more.

The other gulf was an intellectual one. Betty knew she was smarter than her husband. She'd known that from the day of their first after-church coffee. It was a couple of years into the marriage when it struck her that this gulf really kept them apart. She read newspapers and books; he read magazines with lots of pictures. She watched talk shows, he watched comedies, and eventually, when television morphed to that, reality TV. She wanted to talk about politics and social issues and the economy. He wanted to talk about the Devils and whether they would make it to the playoffs.

The American people knew her as First Lady of the United States. But all Betty Edsel wanted was to be John Edsel's first lady. That was a campaign she didn't know how to wage. At sixty, she wondered if there was any hope to win it.

She turned off the television and headed to the bedroom. In an hour or so John would lumber in and crawl into bed beside her. She always woke up when he did, ever hopeful that he'd reach over and wrap his arms around her like he'd done in the early years of their marriage. Nowadays it never happened.

###

Not one hundred feet away, John Edsel was sipping an ice cold Bud and watching the Tarheels trounce his beloved Devils. In some ways, White House home life was damned fine — with waiters delivering his Jack Daniels and emptying his ash trays, a tech staff to make sure the Devils games were recorded when he couldn't watch live, the bed always perfectly made, and never having to take a phone call he didn't want. The only thing missing was that girl who sat in the front row in Sunday School class at Sandy Springs Baptist Church. Part of the problem was time. As governor virtually every minute had been scheduled. As president the schedule was more intense. There was no time for him and Betty to hang out and catch up with one another, except for those damned dinners with the servants buzzing in and out with that healthy food. What conversation they had went nowhere fast. He knew she was a helluva lot smarter than him. When he said something dumb she'd laugh and hug him. Nowadays all she wanted to talk about was government and Europe and Asia and the next election. When she did bring up something personal, like that comment about their bed back in Alabama, it was damned awkward. Was he supposed to talk to her, with the waiter hovering around, about why they didn't have sex any more?

Maybe this wasn't about the pressures of his job. Maybe this was what happened when you were married too long. Maybe this is why men his age got divorced, something that was off the table given that Betty's father was his biggest backer. Actually, the decision to run for office hadn't been entirely his. Jackson Evans made it for him. The old had long wanted to run for governor of Alabama, but he didn't think he could afford to take the time away from his business. By the time Deep-South Machinery was booking five hundred million dollars in annual sales, her dad was almost eighty, too old to hit the campaign trail. So he set a new goal for himself — growing the company to one billion dollars in revenue before he died. Edsel knew Jackson Evans wanted to realize both ambitions through his son-in-law.

He was surprised when old man Evans approached him about running for lieutenant governor of Alabama. The only office he'd ever sought was vice president of the local Rotary. He didn't know a damned thing about government or politics. Not to worry, Evans assured him, we'll hire you a staff that will take care of that. What we need is a man with charisma, a man with personality, a star athlete! It was that final pitch that won Edsel over. He joined a Republican ticket that included the incumbent governor, a man distinguished more by his looks and bright smile than any political initiatives. The Democrats complained that under him, the state hadn't progressed in the past four years. The governor responded that it hadn't fallen either. Edsel, however, knew that the United States of America would have had to have added a fifty-first state for Alabama to slip from its standing, by any measure, on the bottom of the republic.

The campaign had been more fun than Edsel expected, reminding him of nothing so much as the year the Devils were fighting for the NCAA championship. Sure, he had to make speeches. But someone else wrote them, and Edsel routinely declined to answer questions from those annoying reporters. Then he pressed the flesh, something he'd enjoyed during his years as Mid-Alabama Tech's star quarterback. Nothing thrilled him more than bending down to offer an autograph to a little boy or girl or watching a college girl scream and smile and jump up and down, her breasts rising and falling in excitement, as Edsel approached. With John Edsel on the ticket, incumbent Governor Roy Parton stunned the pollsters, winning the election with an unprecedented sixty-six percent of the vote. Edsel walked into the state house in Montgomery on inauguration day, ready for a job that delivered a decent paycheck and required nothing more than showing up for the occasional chamber of commerce banquet. For a moment, it also seemed as if he had won Betty again. On election night, tired as they both were from sitting up and listening to the returns come in, they crawled into bed and made a fierce and passionate love that reminded him of their college days.

It was two months into the new administration when Edsel got the early morning visit from the chairman of the state Republican Party, accompanied by two Alabama State Troopers who were part of Governor Parton's security team. Governor John Parton was dead. Long live Governor John Edsel! Parton's death was billed as a heart attack. The public didn't know the heart attack was precipitated by Parton's habit of inhaling glue from a paper bag. Now Edsel had new insight into Parton's fascination with model airplanes, dozens of which dangled from the ceiling in his otherwise non-descript office. Edsel's new job brought him closer than ever to his father-in-law, who explained that Edsel would inherit a share of Deep-South Manufacturing and retire a wealthy man if he would help Jackson Evans realize his goal of reaching a billion dollars in sales. John Edsel felt like nothing so much as a political linebacker, quietly throwing his considerable government weight around on behalf of the man who was going to make him rich. But the job didn't bring Edsel any closer to Betty. The wild and crazy love they made on election night was never to be repeated.

CHAPTER 12

SATURDAY, FEBRUARY 29
THE FEDERAL SUITE
THE HAY-ADAMS HOTEL
WASHINGTON, DC

Six a.m.!?! What the? London reached across the blanket to press the off button on a clock whose steadily rising alarm sounded like nothing so much as the squad car siren that had heralded her impending arrest in Los Angeles so many weeks ago. It was her first morning in what London suspected was the most boring city in the universe. Los Angeles was about entertainment. Miami was about nightlife and the beach. Washington was about government? Where was the fun in that? A life in Washington, DC, albeit a brief one, was not something London Comfort had ever envisioned growing up in Bel Air. From the age of seventeen she'd been single-minded. She graduated from high school knowing she was going to be a celebrity. She knew her star would shine across a broad universe, and it would sit in that galaxy known by the world as Hollywood, not in Washington, D.C.

For London, growing up hadn't been as easy as her constantly refreshed set of bff's might have imagined. Yes, there was a household staff to make the beds and do the laundry and cook the meals and drive the cars and walk the dog. London had all the clothes she could ever want. She'd never heard of a clothing allowance until she entered University High School, where her father sent her in the hope she'd learn how ordinary people lived. "You mean you only have a certain amount of money to spend on clothes?" she'd asked a high school friend, Rachel Moss, when Rachel bitched that she couldn't afford a new Vuitton bag. London bought what she wanted, and there was more than enough closet space to house her purchases in the Bel Air home her father had purchased the year she was born. The house, at thirty thousand square feet, was a fraction of Aaron Spelling's famous Holmby Hills mansion. It was when London asked her mother why they didn't live in a house as big as the Spellings' that she first learned there was another way the Comforts differed from the families who showed up at the University High School PTA meetings. They needed to keep a low profile, her mother said. It was "complicated."

"Complicated" was London's mother's way of saying that the Comforts were Arabs. Arab was a term London had learned on her abrupt flight to Saudi Arabia after 9/11. The word didn't come up again until junior high school, but London, not known for her prowess in world history, hadn't bothered to read the textbook chapter on the Middle East. It seemed a lot of people didn't like Arabs, unless, of course, they had lots of money. London's father, her mother explained, had come from a moderately wealthy family. Even then he experienced rudeness and discrimination in his early years in the United States. Acceptance came after he changed his Arabic last name to Comfort, sold his first chain of discount motels for two hundred million dollars, and began to build a chain of luxury hotels that he took public for many hundreds of millions more. Still, London's mother explained, she and London's father had decided it would be wise to keep a relatively low profile in a country suffused with anti-Arab bigotry. A thirty thousand square foot house? Yes. A fifty-six thousand square feet mansion? No.

"So because we're Arabs we're a minority?" London asked her mother. "Like Mexicans?"

Her mother slapped her across the face so hard that London almost fell out of her chair. Years later, she could still feel the sting. Arabs, London now knew, were not Mexicans.

The conversation about her Arab origins was one of only a few that London had with her mother growing up. A nanny had raised her. She didn't join her mother and father for meals except for Sunday dinner on those rare occasions when her father was home. Otherwise she ate by herself in the small dining room off the kitchen, served by Mariel, the Mexican housekeeper. High school friends talked about their mothers' awkward attempts to explain menstruation and sex. Neither were subjects London's mother raised. It fell to Mariel to try to explain all that.

For a girl whose public image today was based on her sex appeal, London was remarkably shy and chaste in her early teens. She didn't have a boyfriend. She didn't have many friends at all — just Betty and Rachel, neither of whom was especially attractive but both of whom shared with London, and let her share with them, their dreams and fantasies and fears. It was Betty and Rachel who told London that she was beautiful, something London hadn't seen and resisted believing until her friends hammered the idea into her. Her mother, who rarely spoke with her about anything personal, never commented on her looks. She never asked if she was dating anyone or found any boys attractive. Her father? He adored his daughter. But he travelled constantly, and London was lucky to spend an hour with him each month.

Her mother's distance narrowed when London was finishing her junior year of high school. That May her portrait was prominently displayed in a Los Angeles magazine feature about a local charity. "LA's New Young Beauty," the headline read. Suddenly her mother began to talk with her. Not talk with her really, but take the time to introduce London to her friends at cocktail parties and to engage one of Hollywood's leading photographers to take her portrait. This newfound attention didn't make London feel loved. As a little girl she knew she'd been an inconvenience to her mother, something her mother produced at her father's behest. Now, as a teenager whose beauty was remarked on by everyone she met, her mother saw her as another valuable possession, like the Rodin sculpture in the foyer or the ten-carat diamond ring on her left hand. The boys in high school also started coming on to her, and it was quickly clear to London that they weren't looking for love so much as the right to brag that they'd fucked a girl like her.

London sank into a deep depression halfway through her senior year of high school. With school over, she realized, Betty and Rachel, her only friends, would be off to college. They would be attending Ivy League universities, schools to which even Ali Comfort's millions couldn't buy London admission. In any case, London didn't want to go to college. Studying bored her. But was there an alternative to facing a life without her only friends, surrounded by boys interested only in her body, and a mother who wanted to put her in a glass case and show her off to the friends she wanted to impress? A life like that was enough to make a girl want to kill herself, and for a week in December London gave the idea some serious thought. One morning near the end of that month, a month in which she had struggled to get out of bed, London woke up suffused with an energy and determination so unusual that it alarmed her. Suddenly, her mind was brilliantly clear. The boys in school and her mother objectified her. They wanted to use London's beauty and profit from it in their own personal ways. Why, London asked herself, couldn't she profit from her beauty? If anyone was going to package London Comfort and present her to the world as an object of lust and beauty, why couldn't it be London Comfort?

She called Betty and Rachel, and they joined her in the game of inventing London Comfort the Celebrity. Kim Kardashian and Paris Hilton and Lindsey Lohan had done it, why couldn't she? Rachel and Betty took to the assignment as though it were a crucial final exam. In a month they had helped her craft the profile of the London Comfort the whole world would soon know — a girl whose feigned stupidity was calculated to add a frisson of Marilyn Monroe to an undeniably stunning body. Rachel's father, a screenwriter, loved the idea of creating a celebrity from scratch, something the old studio system had been famous for. He added Roberto Diaz, the publicist, to the brainstorming mix. Betty and Rachel helped London find clothes so provocative that she initially was embarrassed to step out of the dressing room for their appraisal. Roberto introduced her to LA's star-studded nightlife, coaching her on the importance of not arriving at any club or event too early and never being the last to leave. He even shared with her his own directory of city hipsters, with brief bios of the latest iterations of Zooey Deschanel, Ryan Gosling, Elijah Wood, and dozens more in alphabetical order.

In a manner of months, a star was born.

Six years later, there were times when London had trouble remembering which was the real London Comfort and which was the celebrity she and her friends had created with such glee and imagination. The reality TV series that launched her career, depicting her as a party girl with a wild sex life, repelled female columnists for The New York Times and The Wall Street Journal and commentators on PBS talk shows, who claimed she was a young woman being used by the celebrity culture. For London and her publicist, shocking the media establishment was the idea. At first the naturally shy London had to work to make that image seem real. She considered it her toughest bit of acting. Eventually, however, the partying and sexual escapades came naturally to her. The entertainment websites and magazines and TV shows added other elements to the London Comfort persona, painting a somewhat contradictory picture of a young woman who was dumb, which London's handlers were convinced would amp her sex appeal among young men, and yet driven, which they saw as appealing to an older and middle-class female audience. London knew for sure that she was driven, and sometimes she feared she really was dumb. That despite Rachel and Betty's assurances over the years that failing a high school physics or world history class, which she didn't care about anyway, couldn't be equated with a lack of intelligence. Still, London wondered if her arrest on the 405 wasn't proof that maybe Entertainment Tonight had it right and Rachel and Betty had it wrong.

There was a rap on the door, and Kameela entered, fresh, London imagined, from the first of her five daily prayers. It was Saturday. Usually on Saturday London was going to bed at six a.m. This White House gig was going to be rough.

"Good morning, ma'am," Kameela said, correcting herself as London shot her a hard look: "Good morning, London."

"If you say so, Kameela," London said. "I can't believe I'm getting up at this God-awful hour. Got to get dressed and go to the White House to meet this Locke Jones guy and some other guy. I think he's a cop who guards the President."

After a quick shower, London sat in front of mirror to apply her KissKiss Gold and Diamonds lipstick, which at sixty-two thousand dollars a tube was the only purchase her accountant routinely lectured her about, while Kameela dried her hair.

"Do you want me to go with you?" Kameela asked.

"I don't think they'll let you inside," London said, unfolding the papers that had been delivered the night before explaining how to get into the White House. "I'm gonna be there until nine or ten a.m., they tell me. So just order some breakfast and relax. Then when I'm back we'll explore Washington and do some shopping."

Kameela escorted London through the thicket of photographers camped outside the Hay-Adams and across Seventeenth Street to the White House security gate, where she in fact was denied entry, and her burka raised some Secret Service eyebrows. She surrendered her charge and returned to the hotel.

As the security guard guided her to what he called the West Wing, London noted that the White House was as boring as she had imagined. It looked like some sort of old folks home. A nice old folks home. But an old folks home nevertheless. She was seated in a small office, not even as big as her dressing room in Bel Air. In less than a minute, the door opened and in walked a handsome man who London guessed couldn't have been more than thirty-five. His shoes were Gucci, his suit was too, his haircut had to have cost at least one hundred fifty dollars. London knew immediately that he played on Roberto, Howard, and Ralphie's team. The paparazzi at the airport and the hotel and now a queer in the White House. Washington was looking more and more like Hollywood every day. Stepping in immediately behind him was another handsome man, also in his thirties. His suit? London guessed a Macy's house label. His shoes? Maybe Bostonian. His buzz cut? London imagined a corner barbershop. This one was batting on her team. For the first time that morning, London smiled. She felt a flash of heat run through her body, a welcome sensation in this chilly White House office.

"Good morning, Miss Comfort. I'm Lockehart Jones," said Mr. Gucci, extending his well-manicured hand. "And this is Jack Northern. You can call me Locke. Welcome to the White House."

The men settled around the table, as business-like as London's accountant. Locke Jones began to give London the first clear description of what her life for the next three months would be like. As she had feared, each day would start at eight a.m., although thankfully the workweek was Monday through Friday. London was always to dress in what Jones called a "demure fashion," which meant a loose blouse and a skirt that at least touched the top of her knees. That would have to be on her afternoon shopping list. Then there was what Jones called etiquette. While London could call Jones "Locke" and Northern "Jack," the President was always to be addressed as "Mr. President." The First Lady was always to be addressed as "Ma'am." Ma'am! Not only are these people old, London thought, but they want to be treated like they are. The weekends? London was expected to check in with Jones, who would approve her evening plans. She always, always, was expected to be in bed at the Hay-Adams by midnight. In bed alone, Jones added, for emphasis. London's fantasy that Washington, DC, was Hollywood East quickly vanished.

"But what do I actually do?" London asked, when Jones had finished his do's and don'ts.

"Well," said Jones, looking nervously at Northern. "Your duties are going to evolve, which means we haven't entirely figured that out. For starters, you will report to me. I want you to check in with my assistant or me when you arrive each morning. If you can't find us, check in with Jack here, who is always outside the door to the President's office. Then I believe the First Lady will want to begin explaining the White House to you. We're hoping that you could lead some tours. Matter of fact, we've talked to your agent about maybe having you lead a tour for MTV."

At that, London brightened. "MTV? That would be soooo cool! I was worried that my fans would miss me while I'm here."

"By the way, the President and the First Lady would like you to join them for dinner a week from Monday at eight p.m." Jones said. "Now Jack here will show you around the floor." In a flash he was out the door.

"Welcome, Miss Comfort," said Northern, who to this point hadn't said a word. "Follow me, and I'll show you around."

"Please, just call me London," London said. "And I can call you Jack?"

Northern smiled.

An hour later, London Comfort knew the layout of the West Wing's second floor. She'd also spent ten minutes examining the Oval Office. It was the only part of the White House that impressed her. That fireplace on the north end, the door leading to a garden, were very cool. The furniture, a bit stuffy for London's taste, was undeniably expensive and luxurious. It was, Northern told her, the office of the most powerful man in the world. There was only one thing that went unexplained, one thing that struck London as unusual about a place where clearly no expense had been spared to create someone's idea of perfection.

"That stain on the sofa?" she said. "What's that about?"

Northern grimaced and nudged London out the door and into the West Wing hall.

"Let me walk you back to your hotel," Northern said. "We have word that there are photographers outside, and that might be a little uncomfortable. I know a way out of here, and a way into the Hay-Adams, a tunnel that's a lot more private."

Back at the hotel, Jack Northern escorted London Comfort to the front door of the Federal Suite and politely declined her invitation to come in and join her for a drink. As he turned to walk to the elevator, he checked his watch. Nine a.m., and this one was drinking already! Northern sighed. People thought his job was protecting the President from gun-wielding assassins. The assassins he had to be on the watch for were those aiming for John Edsel's character. That, Northern had come to realize, was a very easy target.

CHAPTER 13

SATURDAY, FEBRUARY 29
US HIGHWAY 50 WEST TO ARLINGTON

For a Saturday morning, the traffic was surprisingly heavy on Jack Northern's drive home to Arlington from the White House. What should have been an eight-minute trip was stretching to thirty. Northern had been assigned to John Edsel eight months earlier, when Edsel won the Republican presidential nomination. Before he took the job, he'd started his research because the polls indicated Edsel, beloved of corporate titans, was a shoo-in after he'd agreed to accept Jesse Grant, the African-American who was a Tea Party favorite, as his vice president. What Northern discovered had worried him, although his Secret Service buddies, who had a lot more experience than his twenty-four months, weren't bothered by what he told them. "Remember, America has never elected a President whose middle name wasn't 'Randy'," said Joe Farnam, Northern's boss, who claimed to have stood guard outside President Clinton's office during his encounters with Monica Lewinsky. Besides, Jackson argued, a little sex in the Oval House was easier to deal with than the real craziness that had led GOP leaders to pressure Edsel's predecessor not to seek a second term. Jackson told Northern about the times he'd been called by Madame President's frightened assistant, only to find the leader of the Free World in her office, sobbing uncontrollably with a loaded gun in her hand.

Northern knew the history of sex in high places. Still, Edsel's penchant for online flirtations with teenage girls during the campaign had troubled Northern. It hadn't reached the level of Weinergate, but then Edsel surely knew that pictures of his naked body would be more of a turn off than an allure. There also was the young assistant in the Alabama governor's office, who had "retired" at the age of twenty-one and moved into a mansion on the outskirts of Mobile that had been purchased by Edsel's wealthy father-in-law. What was that all about? And the "housekeepers" who were called at all hours to Edsel's hotel room when he was on the road during the campaign? Edsel himself had told Northern to admit them without an ID check. The fact that they looked like hookers, and that Northern had seen one of them tucking a one hundred dollar bill into her brassiere as she left the suite, made him suspicious.

Northern's suspicions were confirmed shortly after Edsel moved into the White House and Bree Collard was named a White House aide. He quickly realized that only Locke Jones spent more time in private meetings with John Edsel, and Jack Northern was quite certain that the President wasn't gay. His suspicions were confirmed not by evidence, but by the President himself, in a conversation that had made Northern very uncomfortable.

"John, I got something to tell ya," the President had said that day two months earlier, when Bree had run out of the Oval Office in tears.

"Yessir," Northern had responded, standing in a military "at ease" posture in front of the President, who was in his usual position with his feet on his desk. Northern wondered why a man of John Edsel's stature and wealth couldn't get the holes repaired in the soles of his shoes.

"Well, how do I put this?" Edsel had said. "I guess I should start by saying I'm talking to you because I've got more in common with you than I have with Locke Jones." At that Edsel guffawed, and Northern permitted himself a slight grin. Lockehart Jones was the only person in the White House who didn't know that everyone in the White House knew that Lockehart Jones was gay.

The President then invited Northern to take a seat. He needed Northern's help to ensure the privacy of the Oval Office. He needed Northern's help to protect the Presidency — not John Edsel, but the institution. He wanted Northern to talk to Bree Collard and make sure she would keep her mouth shut. The President of the United States was asking Jack Northern to conspire with him to keep his sexual indiscretions under wraps.

To say Northern was conflicted was an understatement. On his drive to his apartment in Arlington that night, he composed in his mind the resignation letter we would tender the next morning. This wasn't what he'd signed up for.

Northern had taken some grief about this job from his parents, who had struggled to supplement the scholarships that had paid for his law degree from Princeton. "Why the Secret Service?" they'd asked. "Why don't you practice law and settle down, and get married, and make real money?" Northern knew his father's disappointment was rooted in status. The owner of a small livery service, Bill Northern had wanted his undeniably smart son to become the sort of man he was used to ferrying to Wall Street from Fairfield County. His mother's biggest worry was that her only child was exposing himself to danger. Northern hadn't examined his reasons for applying for the Secret Service job. But now, as he wondered whether he'd made a mistake, he spent most of the night wondering what he was doing and why. Part of the allure was the quasi-military nature of the job. Northern had mastered the Glock. He'd undergone amazing training that rivaled that of the Navy SEALs. The secrecy also was appealing. Northern had been a fan of spy novels since his teen years. Then there was the sense that he was doing something good for his country. Jack Northern was a patriot, although increasingly a disillusioned one as he found himself closer and closer to the seamy center of American power.

Northern wrote the resignation letter and carefully folded it and sealed it in an envelope for delivery to his boss. But when he got to the office the next morning, the sight of Bree, her eyes still red, her face looking so sad and her slumped body looking so used, stopped him on his way to his boss's office. Northern gestured to Bree and led her into a small room where they could talk in private. An hour and a box of Kleenex later, Northern realized that he probably should have trained as a psychotherapist. He had listened, he had empathized, he had questioned, he had elicited from Bree a promise to keep her distance from John Edsel, and he had coached her on how to do that. By the time he left that room, Northern had decided that his job wasn't so much to protect this particular President, although that was undeniably a priority, but to protect the Presidency of the greatest nation on earth. That was one responsibility on which he and John Edsel could agree. In the weeks and months that followed, and especially as he watched Bree and the President slide back into their affair, Northern knew this was going to be more difficult than merely stopping a bullet.

Northern decided to skip the underground tunnel he'd used to ferry London Comfort from the White House to the hotel. He walked through the hotel lobby and into a crowd of photographers who'd erected a temporary camp on the street. It was a beautiful almost-Spring day in Washington, DC, and the soft breeze reminded him there was a life outside the warren of White House rooms where he spent most of his time. Some day, he promised himself, he'd find time to explore that life, ideally with a woman who looked, but didn't act, like London Comfort. Northern nodded to the security officers at the White House gate, who admitted him without question. He had to hustle now. He needed to oversee the upholstery cleaner he'd engaged to remove that spot from the President's sofa. He had to make sure the guy didn't try to lift any DNA.

CHAPTER 14

SATURDAY, MARCH 7
17TH STREET NW, DUPONT CIRCLE
WASHINGTON, DC

Locke Jones glanced at his cell phone as he walked through the door at Annie's, half an hour early. Unusual for a guy who took pride in being exactly on time, never early and certainly never late. But his obsession with Abdul overrode his obsession with time; Locke couldn't wait to see him. The steakhouse was packed, as Locke expected. Waiting at the bar, he was conscious of being cruised by virtually every gay man around him, and pretty much all the men around him, best Locke could tell, were gay. They were all dressed more casually than Locke, who had so little recent experience in casual settings, or dating for that matter, that he had no idea what to wear on an outing like this. The fact that his jeans were pressed certainly set him apart from the more rumpled crowd around him. His sport coat stood out among the polo shirts. His Gucci loafers were so out of place in a sea of sneakers.

Locke had been a little nervous about making this

reservation. Annie's Paramount Steakhouse was an iconic gay meeting place, the sort Locke yearned to frequent but never dared try except on the rare occasion when he could find a female friend to serve as his beard. Tonight he'd be sitting with Abdul, a man whose good looks would quickly draw the crowd's attention away from Locke. Together, Locke knew, they'd constitute some impressive eye candy, which probably would earn them an awkward and obvious spot at the center of the dining room.

At nine p.m. exactly, Abdul walked in the door. He threw his arms around Locke and brushed his cheek with a kiss.

"Hey mister," he said. "I've missed you."

It was only their fourth meeting in three months, but for Locke, this already had the feel of something that was going somewhere, somewhere intimate, somewhere enduring. Or was that just wishful thinking? They ordered cocktails, Locke again surprised that a Muslim was drinking alcohol. Then again, this was a gay Muslim, a gay Muslim underwear model, so all bets were off when it came to cultural stereotypes.

"So whose briefs and boxers are you modeling these days?" he asked Abdul.

"Well, my little secret is I don't wear any," Abdul said, grinning. "But I think you know that. I only wear underwear when I'm paid to."

The latest campaign had been for the Bjorn Borg underwear line, a brand whose standing was sliding as steadily as its namesake's fame as a tennis star. But if the brand wasn't top of the line, apparently the pay was. Abdul was dressed more casually than Locke, but much more expensively. Locke knew the APO custom jeans with the silver buttons must have cost at least a thousand bucks. The Dior Homme Red Bee polo shirt was another three hundred dollars. And the shoes, by Prada, had to have set Abdul back another thousand. Locke, on a government salary of one hundred seventy thousand dollars, was having trouble keeping himself outfitted in Gucci shoes and shirts and suits — the full Gooch look that he loved.

Dinner was a whirl, with Locke stumbling to recall what he'd eaten as he and Abdul walked into his apartment. His focus had been Abdul, not food, not the crowd. Abdul was a man whose life seemed incredibly glamorous to Locke, a man who lived in a suit, albeit a Gucci suit, surrounded by suits, generally from Brooks Bros., fighting every day for survival in a world where everyone carried a metaphorical knife in his back pocket and couldn't wait to plant it in your back. Abdul travelled the world, with stops in Stockholm, and Paris, and Milan, rather than Tuscaloosa, Detroit, and Tulsa, to recall a few of Locke's recent stopovers. Abdul was admired for his body and his smile and the way he moved on a runway rather than for his ability to give cautious advice on dealing with the Automotive Parts Manufacturers Association or on how to approach the testy chairman of the House Special Subcommittee on Small Business Taxation. Locke knew there were many people who envied his position as Special Advisor to the President, who fantasized about the glamour of working in the White House. Early on, he had drunk that White House Kool-aid himself, but the heady feel of those early days was wearing off and leaving him with a headache. Now he wanted to be himself and not a lackey to the John Edsels of the world. He knew he was good-looking. He wondered if, deep inside, there wasn't a celebrity lurking inside Lockehart Jones, waiting to break out.

Back at Locke's apartment, after fifteen to twenty minutes of passion so intense that Locke thought he might lose his mind, he and Abdul collapsed side by side on the damp and rumpled sheets. Abdul reached into his pants on the floor next to the bed, pulled out a silver cigarette case, and extracted a joint.

"I have to ask you," Abdul said, breathing out the smoke from the first of several hits. "How can you work for that guy?"

"Come again?" Locke said, wondering where this was going and all too aware that smoking marijuana was a violation of federal law.

"John Edsel. Everyone knows the man is dumb. My friends in Europe and the Middle East can't believe the United States of America would pick a man so obviously stupid to be their president."

"Well." Locke froze, unsure how to proceed. "Well, it's a job, Abdul. My job is to make the most of the hand that's dealt me. To do all I can do make the Office of the President work smoothly and efficiently for the people of the United States."

"Come on, Locke. That sounds like you're reading a press release. You're too smart a guy to be working for someone like that. I don't expect you to criticize the man. But you can level with me. Isn't it hard for you?"

Locke took a hit from the joint Abdul offered him. He hadn't smoked one since college. In seconds, all the anxiety, all the tension, faded away. What did he have to fear from Abdul's questions? Intimacy was more than hot sex, Locke reasoned. It was sharing one's hopes and fears. It was asking for help and giving it. Abdul was asking Locke to be intimate with him in a way that went beyond sex. Locke knew he wanted more than sex from Abdul.

"I shouldn't talk about it Abdul. But you're a helluva mind reader. Yes, this is a difficult job. I'm coming off one of the craziest weeks in years."

An hour later, Locke noticed Abdul's eyelids sliding closed and glanced at the clock on the bedside table. It was one in the morning, and he'd been talking nonstop. Abdul, probably jetlagged as hell, had fallen asleep. Locke turned out the light and wrapped his arm around Abdul. But instead of falling asleep himself, his mind began racing backwards through the sixty-minute soliloquy he'd just delivered. Had he really told Abdul about John Edsel's nasty behavior with Bree Collard? Had he really opined that the Edsel marriage was one of convenience? Had he really hinted (he knew he hadn't outright told Abdul the details) that he was involved in mission so important, so secret, so dangerous, that it would call to mind the glorious assassination of Osama bin-Laden? Yes, he had told Abdul all those things. But then Abdul cared about him, and if you care about someone, you keep their secrets. In any case, Abdul was an underwear model. It's not as if the Washington Post would be firing questions at him as he sauntered down the runway at the fall shows in Milan wearing the latest Dolce & Gabbana briefs.

Still, maybe Locke shouldn't have shared all that so soon. Maybe he shouldn't have chanced such a public appearance at as queer a spot as Annie's Paramount Steakhouse with a man Patrick McMullan was sure to photograph if he spotted him. Locke looked at the clock again. It was one thirty now. He needed to get some sleep. He lit the other joint on the nightstand and took a deep breath. There would be plenty of time for reflection, and plenty of time for regret, on Sunday.

Henry E. Scott

CHAPTER 15

MONDAY, MARCH 9
FAMILY RESIDENCE DINING ROOM
THE WHITE HOUSE, WASHINGTON, DC

Before he let her leave the office for her hotel suite and a change of clothes, Locke Jones made a point of counseling London Comfort on dinner, which was at eight o'clock sharp in the Family Residence Dining Room on the second floor, not to be confused, Locke warned her, with the Family Dining Room on the first floor. London was to arrive no later than seven fifty-five, Jones said. Etiquette required that the President and the First Lady always be the last to arrive and the first to depart. If that wasn't confusing enough, Jones also ran through a list of do's and don'ts, elaborating on his advice of Saturday morning. It was "Mr. President" and not "John" or "Mr. Edsel." It was "Ma'am," and not "Betty." Her dress had to reach the middle of her knee — no pants! Only the top button of her blouse could be unfastened. And it should be loose enough to leave something to the imagination. No perfume. She wasn't to ask questions. Her job was to listen and answer whatever questions the First Lady

83

and the President deigned to ask her. And (here London breathed a sigh of relief) it would all be over in an hour.

London rushed back to the hotel, this time skipping the underground tunnel, which required an escort who wasn't immediately available. When she got to the lobby of the Hay-Adams the paparazzi were still camped outside. Cameras flashed, reporters called out her name. London smiled and waved and rushed into the lobby and took an elevator to her suite. Kameela, who had a sense of style completely hidden by that burka, counseled London on her outfit and helped her apply her makeup. Finally, with the clock showing seven forty-five, London stood up from the vanity and looked at herself in the mirror. Who said London Comfort wasn't an actress? She looked as innocent as Mary Tyler Moore.

London was escorted into the Family Residence Dining Room promptly at seven fifty-five, where Locke Jones gave her a quick once-over.

"Perfect," he said, smiling at her for the first time that day.

At eight sharp the butler opened the door to the dining room, and in walked an obviously annoyed Betty Edsel, by herself.

"Miss Comfort, I'm Betty Edsel. Welcome to Washington, and welcome to the White House. The President sends his regrets. There's an emergency he has to attend to."

London was awed by Betty Edsel's regal bearing and surprised herself by offering a slight curtsy.

"Thank you ma'am. I'm delighted to meet you."

Before anyone could utter a word of small talk, butlers had pulled back chairs and a first course was placed in front of each of them. London couldn't take her eyes off the First Lady. Yes, she was old. Yes, the way she dressed was so conservative, with that slightly baggy wool dress. But she had a presence, an aura. It was magnified when she started talking. She didn't talk about herself. She spent the rest of the dinner talking about London, asking her questions, commenting on her television performances. London was dazzled. If only her own mother had shown a fraction of this much interest in her. She found herself telling Betty Edsel about her insecure high school years, even about the campaign she and her friends had concocted to make her a celebrity. Betty Edsel seemed to find every word delicious and kept asking for more.

Finally the dessert arrived.

"So what do you think of our little house?" Betty Edsel asked, her firm voice softened with a slight drawl.

"It's only my second week, ma'am," London said. "But it's beautiful. It's so much bigger than I imagined. There's so much I want to know."

"Well young lady, I think you and I need to spend some time together, if I can pry you loose from Locke Jones. I'm happy to give you a personal tour of this old place, and share some stories about what's gone on behind some of those fancy doors. Stories you won't read in the history books." Betty Edsel winked.

The dessert plates were whisked away and Betty Edsel stood to say goodnight.

"By the way Locke, the President said you were aware of this emergency tonight that kept him from joining us for dinner. What is that about?"

Jones stuttered. There was no emergency that he knew of, and if anyone would know about an emergency, it would be Locke Jones. Then Locke recalled seeing his assistant, the voluptuous Sissy Romero, headed to the Oval Office as he left his office to join London in the Family Residence Dining Room. My God, was he screwing her too?

"Uh, I believe it involved Turkey, ma'am. There was a report about some sort of explosion in the capital there. Rumors that there was a nuclear weapon involved."

"I see," Betty Edsel said. "Well, Ankara is a fascinating city, although obviously I've never been able to get the President to go there with me. I can't wait to chat with him about the situation there. I really haven't kept up to date with what Prime Minister Baykal has been up to. It's amazing, isn't it, that he got elected after that scandal about him having sex with a secretary?"

Locke Jones gulped and rose from the table as Betty Edsel left the room. He had to call John Edsel ASAP.

"She's a piece of work, isn't she?" he said to London as he

darted out the door. "I think she likes you."

London smiled. Maybe this White House gig wouldn't be so bad if she could spend more time with Betty Edsel. If only she'd had a mother like that. She left the White House and walked back across Pennsylvania Avenue, this time flashing an authentic smile to photographers. She was happy. It was amazing how a little interest, a little attention, could warm a soul that, she now realized, had grown so cynical and cold.

CHAPTER 16

TUESDAY, MARCH 10
THE WEST WING, THE WHITE HOUSE
WASHINGTON, DC

London had loved her dinner with the First Lady. The next morning though, she felt like she was back at University High School in West LA, where a toilet stall had been her refuge from teachers who didn't understand that mastery of algebra and world history wasn't required for the life she envisioned for herself, whatever that might be. At University High, however, London could have smoked a joint, something she knew was impossible here in the ladies room on the second floor of the West Wing. At University High, the toilet paper also was much softer and probably more expensive. London glanced at her Tissot. Her brief respite from filing and telephone answering and coffee running for Lockehart Jones was coming to an end. She stood and flushed. As the water stopped rushing and the room grew quiet, she could hear a muffled sound — maybe someone crying? — two stalls over. London stepped to the sink, washed her hands, opened the door to the hall and then loudly closed it without stepping outside. That's when her stall mate, evidently thinking she was alone, let loose. The sobbing, the heaving — it reminded London of that time in sixth grade — before she'd developed the butt, the breasts, the smile that made her the talk of America — when an eighth grader had joked during recess that she looked like a boy.

"Please, can I help?" London stood outside the stall, where the sobbing grew more intense. Then she heard the occupant vomit, and London hoped it was in the toilet.

A flush. Now everything was quiet.

"Are you okay in there?"

The voice was timid, what London imagined a mouse would sound like if a mouse could speak. Then London realized she'd never seen a mouse outside of a cartoon.

"I'm okay. I'm okay. I'm going to be okay." The words were louder now, but the voice quivered.

The stall door opened, and out stepped a young girl, eyes red, makeup drizzling down her cheeks, her blouse disheveled and stained with what looked to London to be eyeliner. Her hair was black, as were her eyes. She was undeniably beautiful. Except for the hair and eye color, and her clothes, which looked as though they'd come from Bloomingdales, and from a sale at that, she could have been London's twin.

"I'm Bree," the young woman said, extending her wet hand to London. "Bree Collard. I work for the President."

"I'm London, London Comfort, and I guess I do too," London said.

"I know," Bree said. "I've heard all about you. You're famous. I couldn't believe I would be working with you."

"What's going on with you? London asked. "Why were you crying? I mean, even if it's that time of month, that was pretty dramatic in there."

Bree looked like nothing so much as a frightened and abandoned puppy. London, surprised at the impulse but unable, maybe even unwilling, to stop it, wrapped her arms around the soiled, wet young girl and hugged her.

"Will you have lunch with me?" she asked. "Then we can talk."

Bree nodded yes. London checked her watch. Damned Locke

Jones probably was outside the door checking his.

"Now I have to run. See you at one p.m. in dining room."

"They call it the Navy Mess," Bree said, smiling for the first time.

"Ugh!" said London. "Whatever!"

As awesome as Monday night's dinner with Betty Edsel had been, London was mired again in the reality of a crushingly boring job. Back at her desk, back at her computer really, since that was where London received and responded to all requests (except for fetching coffee), the emails already were piling up. Most were from Locke, but some were from Susan Sweetzer, the President's secretary, who on Day One had acted as if London belonged to her.

"Please call Secretary Samuels and tell her Locke is running thirty minutes late."

"Call Citronelle and book a table for two in Locke's name at eight p.m. tonight."

"Tell Lydia Crinkle the President won't be able to join the First Lady to meet with Birmingham Mothers for Life this afternoon."

"Call Senator Warnocker and tell him the President would be pleased to meet with him at two p.m. tomorrow afternoon in the Oval Office."

"Come to the President's office ASAP. He wants to meet you!!!!!"

That last message was reinforced by a call from Sweetzer, who seemed annoyed that London hadn't already responded to a message that had just arrived in her in-box. In seconds London was standing in front of Sweetzer, who looked her up and down with her perpetual frown. They have Botox for that, London thought.

"Stand right there. Just a moment. I'll see if the President is ready for you."

Just then the large white door swung open and out stepped

Locke Jones, flashing London a tense smile that she imagined was the mask he wore all day on the job.

"Young lady, come right on in." the President bellowed. "I am honored to meet you, and I am so sorry I couldn't join you for dinner Monday night."

The boom of the command was softened by a Southern accent that added extra syllables to all of the words. "On" was "oh on" and "in" was "e n." Standing there in his stocking feet, his tie loosened and his face glistening with what looked like perspiration, was the President of the United States, all six feet five inches and, London guessed, two hundred fifty pounds of him. His eyes were blue, and they were red, and of course white. Sort of patriotic, London thought. His face was fleshy, especially the jowls, which sagged toward his chest and reminded London of the beagle she'd owned until it chewed up her Louboutins. There was a large mole on his nose, and even from five or so feet away, London would see two small hairs growing from it. The President gestured to a white silk sofa, now devoid of the stain London had seen two days earlier.

"My dear, please have a seat."

"Thank you Mister President."

London perched on the edge of the sofa, careful to keep the hem of the skirt she'd bought on Saturday touching the edge of her knees and folding her hands together in her lap. She'd left unfastened only the top button of this ridiculously blousy blouse. "Demure" was what her acting coach had called that look. While the critics assailed her for being only a celebrity for celebrity's sake, London knew that she was in fact a skilled actress. She could do demure when she needed to.

The President? Well, it was clear to London in the first few minutes of this first meeting that there was no acting there. What you saw was what you got. The man sat in the chair next to her, smiling all the time, his eyes floating up and down her body. London felt as if he were unbuttoning her blouse and then her bra, pulling off her skirt and then her panties. The man made no effort to disguise his appetite.

It was awkward for a moment. London had been told that

she wasn't to speak first when she was in the presence of the President. But he didn't speak either, evidently still trying to process what he was seeing. Finally:

"I just want you to know that we are fans of yours, Miss Comfort, and I am personally delighted to have you with us for the next few months."

"Thank you Mr. President. I am honored to be here. My father is a big supporter of yours. He says the most wonderful things about you."

"Well, I think the world of your father, too. You tell him John Edsel said 'hey.' And if you need anything while you're here, just ask Locke Jones. I've told him to take good care of you. Sometime at the end of week I'd like you to stop by and tell me what you think I could be doing to help the young people in this great country of ours."

At that, the President lumbered up from his chair and extended his hand. London reached out to shake it and was startled to feel him pulling her toward him. A quick kiss on both cheeks, then a tight hug with his right hand clasping her butt. London broke free, her fierce blush showing her surprise.

"That's how those Frenchies do it," John Edsel said. "Now you go on and enjoy your day young lady."

London stepped into the wood-paneled room on the basement level of the White House that they called the Navy Mess. A mess it wasn't. It reminded her of a stuffier version of the Sunset Terrace, that culinary homage to the Fifties back home in LA. She spotted Bree, who quickly flashed her a nervous smile. She'd chosen a table in the corner, where London hoped they could talk without being overheard.

"So, this place is kinda whacked," London said, after the waiter had delivered their order, and it was clear they could move beyond the polite small talk. "I mean, how long have you worked here? Don't you feel like you're in an old folks home? And what's it like working for the President?"

"I love him!" Bree looked as startled as London by what she'd announced. "I mean, I know it's crazy. I know he's an old man, and he's married. But I love him."

At that Bree began crying, and the mascara she'd reapplied only a few hours before began to trickle down her cheeks again. London was relieved that Bree was sitting with her back to the room, which was fairly empty. She reached across the table with her napkin and blotted Bree's cheeks. Then she waved away the approaching waiter.

"Now take a deep breath Bree. You love him? You love that old man? I want you to tell me what this is all about."

By the time Bree ended her story, they'd been at the table for an hour and a half. Both of them would catch hell when they got back to the office. London didn't care. What she was hearing amazed her and appalled her. Every week for almost three months, ever since Edsel Jones has entered the White House, he'd been having sex with Bree Collard. She'd flirted with him, Bree admitted that. She had always been attracted to older men. Besides, the President had told her that he loved her. He told her that sex with her was the best he'd ever had. His wife? That was what he called a "marriage of convenience."

And what was the sex? Bree blushed and shook her head to say no when London asked. London pressed for an answer. What Bree finally described was, by London's measure, remarkably one-sided. Being pushed around and made to service a man? Sure, that could be a thrill once in a great while. A scene like that dominated that damned video Jason had made of her. But a woman had her needs too, and if a man wasn't willing to give as good as he got, well to London he was nothing so much as a john and the woman was no better than a whore. She looked across the table at Bree, who seemed astonished that she'd told London her story. She was undeniably sexy, undeniably beautiful, undeniably young and vulnerable. Anyone, even John Edsel, ought to be able to see that Bree Collard was no whore. It was obvious that she was an emotional twig that could be so easily snapped.

"That man is using you," London said. "I'm sorry. It isn't any of my business. But that old man is using you."

Bree bit her lip, lowered her head, and nodded her agreement.

"I guess I know that." Bree teared up again. "It's taken me so long to realize that London. Somehow, telling all this to you makes it real. I am so pathetic."

"You're not pathetic Bree. You're beautiful. And you're going to tell him to stop. Girl, you're going to take care of yourself. Don't let that old man use you."

Bree nodded her assent as the waiter glided forward to clear the table. Just one week on the job, and London realized she had learned more about politics and government that she ever learned in Mr. Swartz's Civics class.

CHAPTER 17

THURSDAY, MARCH 12
SOMEWHERE IN THE TOBA KAKAR MOUNTAINS, PAKISTAN

The winds were slapping loose pieces of fabric against Abdullah's tent, the tent itself was shaking, and occasionally bits of sand blew through, as if Abdullah needed a reminder of how dry this miserable mountain pass really could be. Abdullah had just finished joining his men in a recitation of the Fatihah, the first chapter of the Koran, as part of his noontime prayer. Now, confident of some privacy, he stretched out on his sand-speckled blanket and reopened the lock on the leather satchel that Ahmed had sent him.

Paris Match, US Weekly, OK, Celebrity Digest, and Hustler, Abdullah's dirtiest pleasure. Abdullah knew these magazines were months old. But as he read them, the world they illuminated, a world he had once lived in, was alive for him. Abdullah leafed through Paris Match, stopping to look at the beautiful women surrounding French President Dominique Strauss-Kahn. He could have been at that reception, if he had made different choices in life. Instead of shivering in a tent on this desiccated mountainside, brushing sand from his sheets, he could have been in a bed at the George V, wrinkling the Frette linens as he made love with one or more French women.

At one time, Abdullah had felt guilty indulging himself with this sort of Western fantasy. Then he heard about the porn videos discovered in Osama bin Laden's Pakistan hideout. Compared to that, he reasoned, this magazine indulgence, even reading Hustler, was minor. The big question, one with which he now struggled every night as he tried to fall asleep, was whether this life of asceticism and revolution was the life he wanted to lead, was the life Allah wanted for him. Abdullah was sure of one thing: There is no God but Allah; and Mohammed is his prophet. Now, isolated and lonely, he found everything else profoundly uncertain. Would the war he was trying to fight ever be won? Would he overthrow the Great Satan? Would Abdullah bin-Salem succeed where Osama bin Laden had failed? Would he end up running a country, as the Ayatollah Khomeini had run Iran? Even if he accomplished all that, would he ever again experience love and passion and, dare he say, fun?

Abdullah glanced again at the entrance to his tent to reassure himself that it was fastened. He opened Hustler and again marveled that there existed a country where such a magazine could be published. When he was working in construction in Pakistan, older friends had shown him copies of Ishtiraq, published in Karachi in the 1970s and popular with college students. Its mix of sex advice columns and poorly reproduced black and white photographs lifted from Western magazines didn't come close to offering the titillation of Hustler. The centerpiece of this issue was an American woman whose body didn't seem up to Hustler's usual standards. For once Abdullah decided to read the story that accompanied the pictures to see if it explained why. The woman was famous because she was a former Republican congresswoman who had become a reality TV star after divorcing her gay husband. Abdullah chuckled — there was so much drama in American life!

The story that really captured his attention was on the pages that followed. It was a guide to Phuket, whose Patong tourist economy was dominated by the sale of sex. There were the clubs on Bangla Road, where Western men drank with beautiful Thai girls. And the hotels, where Hustler claimed room service delivered young women as quickly and easily as it delivered a bottle of wine or a tray of cheese and crackers. Even in his journeys through Paris and London, Abdullah hadn't experienced what Phuket was said to offer. He sighed and set the magazine aside.

Abdullah then picked up US Weekly and stared at the cover. The woman there was beautiful. Abdullah felt an almost-forgotten stirring in his loins that the naked congresswoman hadn't managed to evoke. He flipped to the center of the magazine to read her story — the tale of London Comfort, the queen of celebrity, and her arrest in Los Angeles. Abdullah studied each photo carefully, flipping page by page past the photos of her arrival at a prison, her appearance outside a courthouse, her dancing on the tables at Los Angeles nightclubs. Suddenly he stopped, stunned by the image of London Comfort's father. Ali Comfort, the owner of America' s largest hotel chain. Ali Comfort, father of America's most favorite celebrity? Ali Comfort was Abdullah bin-Salem's brother-in-law. Ali Comfort's mother-in-law and Abdullah bin-Salem shared the same father, if not the same mother, in the wide web of wives and children that Said bin-Salem had woven.

Abdullah flipped through more pages, looking at London Comfort's Bentley, the wrought-iron gates through which one could glimpse the gleaming Ali Comfort mansion in Bel Air, the girls wearing skirts that barely covered their private parts, the nightclub tables with bottles of Dom Perignon. A bit of sand blew into his eye. Abdullah blinked and closed the magazine to rub his eye clean. When he opened his eyes he surveyed the sad interior of his tent and looked again at the photos in US Weekly. Outside he could hear the braying of his donkey. His life and that of Ali Comfort had taken such different directions. Bentley versus donkey. Bel Air mansion versus mountain tent. Dom Perignon versus the revoltingly green Pakola Ice-Cream Soda that passed for a treat in the Toba Kakar Mountains. More dirt blew into the tent, spraying across the magazine pages. The only sand Ali Comfort was likely to encounter, Abdullah realized, shaking the dirt from US Weekly, was on a private beach at his Malibu house or a trap on the golf course at the Bel-Air Country Club.

It was finally time, Abdullah realized, for Salat al-Istikhara, the Islamic prayer for Allah's guidance. The answer wouldn't be swift. The Prophet, Allah bless him and give him peace, famously said: "Your prayers are answered, unless you hasten, saying, 'I prayed, but no answer came'." Abdullah realized that the answer also might not be what he, in his heart of hearts, really wanted to hear. Another gust of wind and the tent shook. Abdullah carefully put his magazines back in the leather pouch, locking it with the key he kept hidden in his thawb. He unrolled his prayer rug and faced the qibla to ensure his prayers would be directed to the Kaaba in Mecca.

"O Allah, I consult You as You are All-Knowing, and I appeal to You to give me power as You are Omnipotent. I ask You for Your great favor, for You have power and I do not, and You know all of the hidden matters. O Allah! If you know that this matter of whether remaining in the Toba Kakar fighting the Great Satan is good for me in my religion, my livelihood, and for my life in the Hereafter, then make it easy for me. And if you know that this matter is not good for me in my religion, my livelihood and my life in the Hereafter, then keep it away from me and take me away from it and choose what is good for me wherever it is and please me with it."

Finished, Abdullah rolled up and put away his prayer rug and stretched out on his mattress, ignoring the gritty sand that permeated the cotton wadding. He smiled. He had faith in Allah, the only God, creator of the universe, and the judge of humankind. It might take a month. It might take a year. But in his heart of hearts, Abdullah bin-Salem believed that Allah would reward him with the life he now was certain he wanted. Abdullah knew that Allah would want him to create life rather than destroy it, to bring the world to Islam by finding women with whom to create more Muslims rather than destroying more heathens. What better place to do that than London, or Paris, or — here Abdullah smiled again — Phuket?

CHAPTER 18

MONDAY, MARCH 16
THE EAST WING, THE WHITE HOUSE
WASHINGTON, DC

London Comfort was waiting when Betty Edsel arrived at her office at eight a.m. Today the First Lady was going to give her a personal tour of the White House, with the idea that London might soon be conducting her own for school children who, the First Lady's press secretary hoped, would be as awed by her celebrity as much as the grandeur of the rooms. There was a hint that an MTV special might also be in the offing. They started in the Blue Room, which, as its name would suggest, was festooned with blue drapes and anchored by a massive blue carpet. The furniture, Betty Edsel explained, was from the time of President James Monroe in the early 1800s. Then they moved to the Green Room, where the walls as well as the curtains were green. Next was the Red Room, also with an early 1800s decor, with red walls that London thought were funereal. The enormous East Room, with its off-white walls and enormous chandeliers, was a welcome relief from the oppressive gloom of the rest of what the

First Lady described as state reception rooms. It was here, she explained, that the President received other world leaders, and the East Room was where they threw the occasional party. The State Dining Room, the bowling alley, the Lincoln Bedroom, the Queen's Bedroom, the Map Room, the Diplomatic Reception Room, the Vermeil Room, the China Room, the Library. London's parents' house in Bel Air seemed miniscule in comparison. She scribbled notes as quickly as she could despite Betty Evans' kind offer to provide her with a briefing book to prep for leading her own tours. London also peppered the First Lady with questions and was impressed that she never lacked an answer.

"Which President built this room? When was this wing added? Who built the portico? Who is that portrait of? What is the style of that furniture? What does that image in the carpet mean?"

London felt as if she were prepping for a final exam that she wanted to pass with flying colors. She didn't know why, but she wanted to impress this woman, something she'd never felt with any high school teacher.

Finally they returned to the East Wing and Betty Edsel's office.

"So young lady, I'm impressed," Betty Edsel said.

"Ma'am?" London asked.

"By your questions, your curiosity, your energy. I must say, all of that contradicts your public image, and in a very nice way." Betty Edsel smiled.

London Comfort knew it was vapid, but "awesome," was the word that came to mind as she looked at her tutor. The woman was awesome. Yes, she was sixty years old. But her hair was so perfectly coiffed, with beautiful strands of silver streaked through the black. Her posture was amazing. She sat on the sofa in her office, her torso erect, her head held high, her chin raised. Then there was that wry smile. It seemed as if everything amused or fascinated Betty Edsel.

"So, what can I tell you about the White House that you haven't learned today?" Betty Edsel asked.

London had questions, but she wasn't sure if she should ask them. Two days before, in preparation for this tour, she'd asked Kameela to go to a bookstore and see what she could find about White House history. Kameela brought back a stack of books on its architecture, its interior, its grounds. But the book that captivated London was one about its inhabitants. There was Thomas Jefferson, who had an affair with Sally Hemings, his slave. There was Grover Cleveland, whose bastard child gave rise to a chant by opponents of "Ma, Ma, Where's My Pa," during his campaign appearances. (Cleveland's supporters had responded with a gusty "Gone to the White House, Ha Ha Ha!"). There was Warren Harding, who carried on two long-term affairs and fathered an illegitimate child. There was Franklin Roosevelt and Lucy Mercer. There was Dwight Eisenhower and Kay Summersby, whose relationship at least pre-dated his inauguration. There was John F. Kennedy and Marilyn Monroe and Judith Exner, to name two of possibly many lovers. There was Bill Clinton and Monika Lewinsky. Finally, there was John Edsel and Bree Collard. London hoped the wonderful woman in front of her didn't know about that.

Was it this house, grand yet isolating? Was it this job, powerful yet all-consuming? Was it the sense of power? London expected this behavior from Jason and the boys she played with in LA. But these were adult men, smart men, accomplished men, powerful men. Could it be that this was just what men did, what men were? The thought depressed her.

"Ma'am, I hope this question isn't inappropriate, but I wonder if you could tell me about some of the men who governed from here. Grover Cleveland, Warren Harding, Franklin Roosevelt, Dwight Eisenhower, John Kennedy, Bill Clinton. I mean, why?"

Betty Edsel knew her American history and understood immediately what London Comfort was getting at. If she had been taken aback by the question, she didn't show it. She still had that bemused smile on her face as she essayed an answer.

"London, I don't think we'll ever know why men do what they do," the First Lady said. "Certainly all men don't cheat on their wives. And I don't think Presidents are more likely to do that than other men.

"As you grow older, young lady, I suspect your expectations of love will change. You may always expect and want fidelity. If that's so, I hope you find it. You might also come to believe that a man can give you a lot of attention and support and companionship — what I call love — and still have sex with other women. I don't think there's a right way or a wrong way. We each have to decide what we can live with."

Now, for the first time that morning, the wry smile faded from Betty Edsel's face. She looked down at her hands, the fingers of her right one turning the wedding and engagement rings on her left one.

"There also is the man who, whether he is sleeping with other women or not, can't or won't give you the love and attention you want and need. That kind of marriage, in my opinion, is always wrong. There are women who stay in such marriages, for the money, for the prestige, for their children. But life is too short young lady. It's too short for a woman of sixty, like me, and it's also too short for a woman of twenty-six, like you. Both of us deserve better. Both of us deserve to live lives full of meaning and love and respect."

At that, the First Lady bounced to her feet and smiled broadly.

"Now it's time for you to get back to that dismal desk job, and for me to review the menus for some upcoming White House dinners. Be patient, in a week or so we'll have you out of Susan Sweetzer's clutches and over here, working with me. London Comfort the Hollywood celebrity will be London Comfort the White House celebrity."

Betty Edsel stepped forward and gave London Comfort a hug. London, her eyes tearing up, headed back to her desk in the West Wing.

CHAPTER 19

MONDAY, MARCH 16
DYNASTY APARTMENTS
ADAMS MORGAN
WASHINGTON, DC

By the time Bree Collard arrived at her apartment in Adams Morgan, it was seven-thirty. Another long day at a job that paid very little and now, Bree was beginning to believe, cost very much. After a quick shower, she turned on the television. There, on Access Hollywood, they were talking about London Comfort. Some guy named Jason had a tape of her? People were trying to buy it from him? They were talking about London like she was some snotty bitch. That wasn't the London Comfort that Bree Collard saw. This Jason guy called her a "ball buster," a woman who wouldn't take crap from anyone. That, Bree thought, was more like the London she was getting to know.

She had to admit that London was right about the President. He was using her. Really, what chance was there that he'd divorce that rich old wife of his and marry her? Bree didn't know much about politics, but she knew that would shake the nation.

She'd heard rumors that he'd fooled around with another intern when he was governor of Alabama. And Sissy Romero, the assistant to Locke Jones, she seemed to spend an unusual amount of time in the President's office. Was he screwing her too?

Why was she so in love with this man? It really did feel like love. The President was all Bree could think about. At least once a week, he called her into his office, winked at that nice Secret Service agent, closed the door and kissed her so deeply and passionately that even now, thinking about it as she lay on her new Ikea sofa, Bree could feel herself growing moist. She'd never had a man in her life like that. Sure, there were the boys in high school and at Wake County Community College back in North Carolina. But there really wasn't much to them. They were small, they were silly, they were dumb. Edsel Jones, he was like a daddy to Bree, and Bree had never had a daddy — well, she hadn't met her real daddy, and her mother wouldn't talk about him. When the President wrapped those big arms around her, Bree wanted to be his little girl forever.

Once he was done with her though — well, that was a different story. Basically, he threw her out of his office. No goodbye kisses. Not even a gentle hug. He got off, and he was on to the next thing, and the next thing wasn't Bree Collard. Yes, she was being used. She'd seen a Dr. Phil show about this. She'd seen an Oprah show about this. London Comfort was right. Bree had to put a stop to it. What would happen, she wondered, if she just said "no"? Would she get fired? Would she be moved to another job? Bree needed the job. She had college loans to pay, and her mother didn't have any money. It had crossed her mind to try a Monica Lewinsky. Maybe she could make some money and become a celebrity too. Bree had no idea how to go about that. Besides, it seemed so mean, so cruel, to do to John Edsel what Monica Lewinsky did to Bill Clinton. But then wasn't John Edsel being mean to her? Wasn't he being cruel? Another picture of London Comfort flashed across the TV screen. Bree smiled. If anyone knew how to turn Bree's situation into celebrity, it was London Comfort. Bree headed to the refrigerator for a bowl of chocolate ice cream. She could worry about her waistline later.

The next afternoon Bree got a text from Susan Sweetzer. The President wanted to see her. ASAP! She knew what this meant. The old man was horny. What she didn't know was how she was going to handle it. Last night she'd gone to bed resolved to put John Edsel, Mr. President, in his place, whether or not she lost her job. She would take Jack Northern's advice. Now, in the White House, just steps from the Oval House, Bree Collard's resolve began to fade.

Jack Northern smiled at her when she approached the door to the President's office and, nice as always, he opened it for her. He didn't say anything, but he looked as if he wanted to remind Bree to stand up for herself, to not let herself be used.

"Bree darling." John Edsel was in his shirtsleeves, walking around his office in his socks, his shoes tossed near the sofa. He threw a sheaf of papers on his desk.

"Bree darling, I haven't seen you in a week. How is my little girl doing?"

Edsel approached, his arms wide open, the signal for Bree to rush forward and embrace the man she called Daddy. This time Bree stiffened. She didn't move. Her lips curled outward and down in that universal human signal of doubt and dismay.

"Darling? Is something wrong? Haven't you missed your Daddy? You know all I've done the past week is think about you. I've been so busy, and I've missed you."

Edsel loosened his tie, then he smiled so broadly that Bree could see, from three feet away, the gold fillings in the back of his mouth. It was the smile that Bree found so hard to resist. Her body, her resolve, melted. Edsel stepped forward and embraced her softly, lovingly. Bree felt her heart beat faster. His lips brushed her neck, his tongue probed her ears, then shifted to race lightly across her lips. Bree moaned. Edsel grabbed the back of her head with his thick hand, holding it fast while he pushed his tongue deep into her mouth. With the other hand he was lifting the hem of her skirt and rubbing between her legs.

In a minute, maybe two, Bree Collard was on her knees. John Edsel unzipped and pushed himself into her mouth until she gagged. But he didn't stop. He held the back of her head with both hands now, pushing her forward while he thrust himself into her over and over. Maybe two minutes more, and he groaned. Bree could taste his bitter fluid at the back of her mouth. She stayed for a second on her knees, hoping he would pull her up, kiss her gently, hold her, and tell her he loved her. But no, he was looking at his watch.

"Got an appointment darling. So you're gonna have to go. Come back and see Daddy real soon now, hear?"

The telephone rang and Edsel grabbed it, turning his back to Bree, still on her knees. Her eyes filling with tears, she rushed from the Oval Office to the bathroom down the hall. She spit in the sink over and over and rinsed her mouth. She started to cry, biting the washcloth to mute the sound.

Would she never learn? She so hated John Edsel. She also hated herself. She had let him do this to her. She never would again. She had to talk to London Comfort. This time she also had to listen to London Comfort.

CHAPTER 20

WEDNESDAY, MARCH 18
THE WEST WING, THE WHITE HOUSE
WASHINGTON, DC

"We have to talk."

Jack Northern was taken aback by London Comfort's approach. For once, she didn't have that Valley Girl lilt to her voice. She wasn't smiling seductively either. This wasn't a faux question. This was an order. London Comfort looked as if she was used to getting what she wanted.

"What about?" Northern asked.

"The President," Comfort said. "But this isn't the place. It's damned important. In fact, it's a national security issue. Can we meet outside this weird place?"

"You can't just leave here. Susan Sweetzer and Sissy Romero will be furious."

"Like I give a damn what that shriveled old bitch and that little tramp think. There's no way Sweetzer will be as furious as I am right now at John Edsel. If your job is protecting the President of the United States, you need to talk to me. Now."

Northern texted his backup, who was down the hall. In seconds the man was there to take Northern's place outside the Oval Office door.

"Where should we go?" Northern asked, surprised to realize that London had taken charge.

"Back to my hotel room, through that tunnel of yours. Unless you've bugged my room. Then we're going to have to find someplace else."

"No, no one has bugged your suite. Let's go. But we have to make this fast. I can't be away from my post for long."

In a manner of minutes London and Jack Northern were at the door of the Federal Suite. Kameela responded quickly to London's knock. She whisked London and Northern, clearly startled to see a woman in a burka, into the sitting room and departed.

"So, what is this national security issue?" Northern asked, settling onto the sofa. "And who is that woman in a burka?"

"We'll talk about that woman later, as if it's any of your business," London said, flashing anger. "This is about the President of the United States sexually abusing Bree Collard. Word in the office is he's screwing Locke Jones' assistant too. She's what? Twenty-two? Twenty-three? Now the son of a bitch wants to see me this afternoon. If he so much as touches me I'm going to knee him in the balls. How are you going to protect him from that, Mr. Secret Service?"

Northern's open mouth and raised eyebrows signaled shock that quickly collapsed into the closed mouth and furrowed brow of concern.

"London. My God. I don't know what to say." Northern looked down at the carpet, as if he were ashamed. "I know about his.... Well, I know about some of it. I don't really know the details."

"So, what are you doing about it?" London asked.

Northern sighed.

"I don't know what I can do about it. I talked to Bree. I tried to coach her to say no. But London, he's the President of the United States. He's the boss of my boss's boss's boss. He's the

Commander in Chief. He's the leader of the Free World. I don't know what I can do."

Suddenly London felt sorry for Jack Northern. He clearly was ashamed — not so much of John Edsel, but of his inability to do anything about him, his inability to protect Bree. Her voice softened.

"Jack, you seem like such a nice guy. But you work for such an awful man. It's not just Bree, you know. There's lots of gossip about this guy and what he does to young girls."

Northern, his head down, nodded.

"What good are you doing your country, what good are you doing the Presidency, if you let this happen? I'm not going to pretend I know all about the White House and history and politics. I know the jokes they make about me being a dumb celebrity. I admit I failed social studies and history. But Jack Northern, I know that no one has the right to abuse an innocent young girl, or even a not-so-innocent girl like me."

Northern bit his lower lip and nodded in agreement.

"It's not like I don't agree with you London. I do. I just don't know what to do about it."

"Well I know what to do about it. This dumb celebrity knows what to do about it. But I need your help."

Ten minutes had passed when Northern got a text from his stand-in outside the President's office.

"Where r u? When u coming back?"

He rose from the sofa, and London embraced him. Northern stood there, rigid, not sure how to react. London didn't let go, and Northern felt a stirring in his loins. He looked down at London, who was looking up at him, her lips slightly parted, her tongue expectant. Northern wrapped his arms around London and bent to kiss her. Suddenly he realized how long it had been since he'd been with a woman. He didn't want to stop. He didn't want to let go. Then he heard the beep of another text. He had to get back to work.

Northern escorted London Comfort back through the tunnel to the White House, neither of them speaking. His mind was reeling at the thought of what he'd just agreed to. He'd agree to jeopardize his career, maybe even risk jail. He'd agreed to the sort of radical assault on the President that he was hired to prevent. As amazed as he was about all that, he knew London Comfort had convinced him to do the right thing. Now he knew that there was more to her than he had first imagined, more to her than the celebrity magazines knew. This girl — this woman — as silly and intellectually flimsy as she sounded on reality TV, had a backbone, she had integrity. She also was even sexier in person than she was on TV. Northern looked over at London, walking beside him. She looked at him and grabbed his hand. Northern didn't let go until they reached the door at the White House end of the tunnel, with its video camera. This woman was beautiful; this woman was fierce and principled. This woman might not be so smart, but she was smart enough to know that. Jack Northern wondered: Was he falling in love?

CHAPTER 21

WEDNESDAY, MARCH 18
THE FEDERAL SUITE
THE HAY-ADAMS HOTEL
WASHINGTON, DC

London was exhausted when she pushed open the door to her Hay-Adams suite. It was seven-twenty p.m., and Kameela was kneeling on her prayer rug in the corner of the living room.

"'"Allaahumma salli 'alaa Sayidina Muhammadin wa 'alaa ali Sayidina Muhammadin Kamaa sallaita 'alaa Sayidina Ibraaheema wa 'alaa ali Sayidina Ibraaheema Innaka hameedun Majeed Alaahumma baarik 'ala Sayidina Muhammadin wa 'alaa ali Sayidina Muhammadin Kamaa baarakta 'alaa Sayidina Ibraaheema wa 'alaa ali Sayidina Ibraaheema Innaka hameedun Majeed."

London didn't understand a word of it. But the sound, the cadence, was magical. Kameela prayed for only minutes. After what she'd endured today, the sound was as relaxing to London as an Ativan. At least she'd ducked an encounter with John Edsel. When Susan Sweetzer told her to head to the Oval Office,

London feigned a headache and nausea. It was her period, she'd told Sweetzer, hoping that would keep the dirty old man at bay for a little while.

Finished with her prayers, Kameela stood and smiled at London as she rolled up her prayer rug.

"How was your day? I hope it was a happy one."

"Happy? It was anything but happy Kameela. It was rough. I need your help."

London and Kameela settled on the sofa, London taking Kameela's large black hand into her tiny white one. She sighed.

"Kameela, I know I don't have to remind you. When you signed on to work with me, you agreed to keep everything you saw, everything you heard, everything we did, confidential. You remember?"

"Of course, London. I would never talk about you to anyone."

"I know. I'm only reminding you because I need your help on something very, very confidential. Something that might even be a little dangerous. But it's very important."

London opened her Vuitton handbag and pulled out a stack of one hundred dollar bills. She counted out twenty and put them in Kameela's hand.

"I want you to buy a video camera for me, Kameela. But you can't say who it's for. And, I know this is hard, but you can't wear your burka when you're buying it. I don't want someone to get suspicious, someone to follow you and find out what you're doing."

Kameela nodded her assent, but her raised eyebrows and open mouth signaled London that she wanted to know more.

"Can I ask you why you need this camera London?"

"Yes, Kameela. I am going to videotape the President of the United States trying to rape a girl."

After ordering room service and sharing a meal with London (it turned out the Hay-Adams had a halal menu), Kameela left her charge and returned to her room down the hall. Soon it would be time for Isha, the final prayer of the day. Kameela opened the tiny safe in the closet and tucked the two thousand dollars London had given her under the miniature video camera that Ahmed Azhar had given her two weeks earlier. It was all so strange.

On Monday a week ago Ahmed had called and asked her to meet him at an odd little park a block south of the Capitol. Kameela arrived at the park at nine that morning and made her way to a splashing fountain with the Botanical Garden looming in the background. Ahmed was sitting on the edge of the fountain's pool, as handsome as the day she had met him at the Muslim Women's Association.

"Asalaam Alaykum," Ahmed said, rising from his concrete perch and simultaneously gesturing for Kameela to sit and join him.

"Wa 'Alaykum Asalaam," Kameela responded, thrilled to be in the presence of a man every bit as sexy as Wael kfoury, the now-graying Lebanese singer whose picture every Arab woman friend seemed to have buried deep in her purse. Ahmed's accent amused and intrigued her. It reminded her of the white men she knew back in Charlotte.

"Kameela, Allah and his prophet Mohammed, peace and blessings be upon him, have a mission for you. It will be difficult, and it will be risky. But it is so important to Allah and to Islam."

At that, Ahmed reached into his black leather shoulder bag and removed a small box that he placed on the edge of the fountain between them.

Kameela was flattered, and she was scared. From the day she had first embraced Islam, she knew she had a greater mission in life. Her advisors at the Women's Association had told her to be patient. Allah would reveal that mission, all in good time. Perhaps this was it. But this box, did it contain a bomb? Would she be asked to sacrifice her life, and the lives of others? This was an aspect of her faith that most troubled her. She knew that Muslim people around the world were subject to vicious bigotry. She'd felt it herself in some parts of LA after she started wearing the burka. Still, it didn't seem right to take the lives of innocent people, even if it was to fight those who were evil. She knew many of her Muslim friends agreed with her on that. Ahmed, watching her intently, pulled the lid off the box and extracted what appeared to be a small camera. Kameela's tense body relaxed so dramatically that it provoked a laugh from him.

"You thought I was going to ask you to plant a bomb?" he asked, smiling. "No. I'm just asking you to take some pictures."

"Pictures?" Kameela smiled, relieved. "Of course. Pictures of who?"

"Pictures of the President of the United States. Pictures of him having sex with young women who are not his wife."

Kameela stiffened again.

"But. The President of the United States? How? I've never even been inside the White House. How do I take pictures of the President of the United States?"

"That we still have to figure out," Ahmed said. "I'm hoping that London Comfort can help you. You see, we have a video of her that she will find very embarrassing. But if she could help us get a video of John Edsel, one that will be even more embarrassing, we can make that video of her disappear."

Kameela took the camera and tucked it into her burka. She had never imagined something like this as the mission Allah had in mind. This was going to take some thought.

"Ma'assalama," Ahmed said, standing up to take his leave. "I'm headed over to tour the Capitol."

"Go in peace," responded Kameela, who stood and watched as Ahmed walked away. As he receded into the distance, she tried to remember the last time she'd had sex with a man. Certainly not since she'd donned the burka. Her friends at the Women's Association had talked about finding her a husband. It seemed they had candidates. Kameela wasn't sure. As much as she missed the thrill of sex and the comfort of a man in bed beside her, she still was wary of the potential for violence and drama that had characterized her earlier relationships.

Ahmed now had faded from sight, and Kameela started walking back to the Hay-Adams. Suddenly she stopped. Ahmed had said he was going on a tour of the Capital, which was north of where they had met. Ahmed had walked south. What was that about? Maybe nothing. Still, if she was going risk her life to spy on the President of the United States for Ahmed Azhar, maybe she ought to know a little more about him and what he was up to.

A five-minute brisk walk, and Kameela spotted Ahmed ahead of her, finishing a cigarette outside the entrance to a curved beige building on South Capitol Street. Ahmed tossed the cigarette to the sidewalk and crushed it under the heel of what looked to be an expensive shoe. Then he pivoted toward the entrance of the building and walked through the glass doors. The sign above them read "Democratic National Headquarters."

CHAPTER 22

WEDNESDAY, MARCH 18
BANYAN APARTMENTS
ARLINGTON, VA

It was eight p.m. when Jack Northern pulled into the parking lot at his Arlington apartment building. Most of his days were, he had to admit, boring. This one had been anything but. It had been upsetting, exhilarating, frightening, confusing. First was the meeting with London Comfort, then he'd been summoned into the President's office.

"Congratulations, young man," John Edsel had said, his voice sounding as always as if it were broadcast from a loudspeaker. "I told the Secretary of Defense that I want you to be part of the team that's going to capture Abdullah bin-Salem!"

"Mr. President, I don't know what to say. Thank you."

Edsel slapped him on the back.

"You're welcome Jack. I have confidence in you. I'm counting on you to capture that terrorist. I'm also counting on you to save my ass while I'm in this job. Not just from assassins with guns, but those with the TV cameras. You know what I mean." John

Edsel winked.

Northern, who had asked earlier if he could join this mission, soon would be flying across Pakistan with some of the nation's most talented military operatives. As anxious as he was — actually, he had to admit, as frightened as he was — he was thrilled to have landed the assignment. It was important. It had meaning. He was to help the SEALs capture the greatest living threat to the security of the United States of America. If only his mother and father knew what their son was about to do. Of course he could never tell them. If ever there was a state secret, this was it. That was a shame, because he couldn't imagine an accomplishment of which they'd be more proud.

Edsel's announcement gave Northern pause as he thought about working with London to plan the President's downfall. Had he really just agreed to secretly videotape a sexual assault by the President of the United States? What would they do with the video, once they had it? London had told him not to worry; she had PR folks who knew how to handle that. Getting a celebrity sex video on the Internet, with follow up coverage on E! the Entertainment Television Network, apparently was a piece of cake. Jack knew it would shake Washington. Hell, it would shake America and the world, except perhaps for France, which greeted such revelations with a yawn. Northern was sure Edsel would have to resign. There was a vice president in place, though, who would quickly take his place. He seemed like a smart and competent guy, although Northern knew little about him. The upheaval was worth it, he reasoned, if it sent a message that America would not tolerate the abuse of women, if it helped restore the dignity and gravity of the office of President of the United States.

The videotape conspiracy and the bin-Salem mission. And then he had kissed America's most famous celebrity in her hotel room. Just what was he getting himself into? Was he fooling himself to think she was as passionate about him as he was about her? Did his passion make sense? Come to think of it, did passion ever make sense? Passion was the antithesis of logic. That's why it wasn't something he had ever let himself yield to.

That's why all those dates in high school and college had been so awkward. He knew women, well most women, found him handsome. He loved being with a woman, loved sex. He was just so damned awkward at it. It was easier to concentrate on his job.

Northern was in bed by nine, with his laptop perched on top of the covers, searching YouTube for videos of London Comfort. "Ten Stars of Celebrity Sex Tapes," "Scary Celebrity Sex Tapes" — Jack was relieved not to find London on either of those. There was, however, an E! Entertainment clip. Northern clicked on it to hear an E! correspondent discuss a rumored video that London Comfort would find very embarrassing if it surfaced. Several scandal magazines had said they would pay big bucks for exclusive stills from that video. The E! correspondent invited anyone in his audience to call if he or she had a copy. No wonder London knew so much about how to get a sex video distributed. Did she also know how to keep one from being distributed?

Northern shut down the laptop and opened the briefcase beside the bed. He stretched out on the bed and began poring through the US Navy SEAL Combat Manual and Sikorsky's explanation of the mechanics of the UH 60, a truly amazing piece of machinery. Northern discounted the rumors that the Defense Department was going to replace the Black Hawk with the Kudzu. The Black Hawk was a Ferrari compared to the Kudzu, which The Times Pentagon correspondent described as an Edsel in an apparent reference to the infamous Ford automobile, although given the President's reputation inside the government for incompetence, it might well have been a reference to him.

Northern was lost in an explanation of the Black Hawk's electronic instrumentation and flight controls when his cell phone buzzed. A text message. It was London Comfort.

"You free to talk?"

"Yep. Give a call."

"I'm downstairs."

Downstairs? What was London Comfort doing in Arlington, Virginia? Northern jumped out of bed and slipped into a pair of jeans crumpled on top of a chest of drawers. How did London Comfort even know where he lived?

"Minute," he texted back. He stepped into the living room, which was a mess, with sneakers scattered across the floor and piles of old newspapers on the sofa. In the kitchen, there were dishes stacked in the sink and the tiny dining table was coated with dust. A far cry from the Federal Suite at the Hay-Adams. A far cry even from a room at Motel Six. But hell, she was outside.

Barefoot and bare-chested, Northern opened the front door. There stood London, smiling like a Girl Scout hoping to sell him a box of cookies.

"I'm sorry to surprise you. I was just. Just. Well. I was wondering if we could talk some more."

"Uh, sure. I mean, how did you even know where I live?"

"Well, I do have access to that White House computer in Susan Sweetzer's office." London smiled. "You think I spend all my time looking up phone numbers of fancy restaurants so I can book dinners for Locke Jones?"

"I'm sorry about my apartment," Northern said. "It's a mess. But honestly, I don't get much company. Well, to be honest, I don't get any company."

London pulled the newspapers from the couch and stacked them neatly on the floor. Then she kicked off her shoes and plopped on the couch, tucking her beautifully manicured feet under her butt. She patted the seat beside her, inviting Northern to take a seat. Northern smiled. This girl knew how to take charge. She was inviting him to take a seat in his own apartment.

"I want you to know it meant so much to me that you listened to me today. I know I was angry. Maybe I was even a little bit out of control. But you were a gentleman. You could have walked out of that hotel room. You even could have called someone and had me sent back to prison. But you didn't."

Northern reached over and took London's hand in his, wondering for a moment if he was being brash. London squeezed his hand and smiled. Then she leaned forward and kissed Northern on the lips, pushing her tongue forward until it engaged his. In a minute they were awkwardly trying to wrap themselves around one another on the sofa. Northern's briefly thought he should disengage. This was getting out of control, and that scared him. But then, he realized, he was thinking logically. That wasn't what passion was about.

"Let's go to my bedroom, okay? It's messy too, but I'll keep the lights off."

"No Jack. I want the lights on. I don't care what I see so long as I see you."

Once in the bedroom they tore at one another's clothes. Soon London was naked, lying on Jack's bed. He stood in front of her, awed by what he saw. Some of the celebrity show videos on YouTube had been revealing. But the real London Comfort was more beautiful, sexier, than Jack Northern could ever have imagined.

Northern crawled across the bed, hovering over London on his hands and knees. He wanted to take his time. He wanted to explore every inch of her body with his tongue, with his lips, with his hands. He wanted to hear her moan. He loved that she didn't close her eyes. Instead she seemed transfixed by his.

Northern was almost finished with his exploration when London took charge again. She wrapped her long and slender legs around his waist and pulled him on top of her and inside her. This time it was Northern who moaned until he finally exploded, both of them making the sort of carnal sounds Northern hadn't heard since college.

Now Northern lay on his back, with London's head on his shoulder and her right hand skimming playfully across his chest.

"So," Northern said, playfully. "We haven't done much talking."

"I don't know what to say," London said. "Or maybe I don't know how to say it. It all sounds so crazy. I mean, I don't really know you. But I feel so connected with you. You seem so authentic. You seem so real. I wasn't sure a man like you really existed."

"You make me blush, London. But I'm also so different from you. You're from Hollywood, and I've never even seen the Oscars. I can tell you're interested in fashion and style. My idea of fashion is that black suit and white shirt I wear to work everyday, and a t-shirt and jeans when I'm off duty. You're so exotic. I'm from small town Connecticut."

London put her finger against Northern's lips to silence him.

"Can we talk more about how we're alike? I'm an actress. What the world sees on TV, what people read in magazines, that's not the real London Comfort. That's a part I play. Yes, I grew up with money, with servants. Yes I stay in a fancy suite at the Hay-Adams where there are people who come to pick up the newspapers on the sofa and the sneakers on the floor. Deep down inside though, I'm just a girl, a girl who wants to be with a boy, with a boy who loves her, a boy she can trust, a boy who isn't always looking over her shoulder to see if a more beautiful girl is coming into the room. I think you're that kind of boy, that kind of man, Jack. I also like that you're smart. I know everyone thinks I'm dumb. That's the image my agent created for me, and it's worked. It's helped me make money so I don't have to depend on my Dad. The truth is, I'm not some intellectual, I didn't go to college. But I'm not stupid. I want to be with a man who doesn't think stupid is sexy."

London stopped speaking and looked at Northern intently, as if seeking some sort of affirmation.

This doesn't make sense, Northern thought. This isn't logical. I hardly know this woman. She's telling me that she isn't what the rest of the world thinks she is. Could that be true? Is she acting again? Why do I believe her?

London caressed his cheek.

But then passion doesn't make sense, Northern remembered again. Maybe it was time to see where passion would take him — the passion London so quickly brought to the surface. He pushed her back onto the bed and rolled atop her, kissing her deeply until she wrapped her legs around him and pulled him inside her again.

CHAPTER 23

THURSDAY, MARCH 19
THE OVAL OFFICE, THE WHITE HOUSE
WASHINGTON, DC

Being President of the United States of American wasn't all it was cracked up to be. There were all those damned speeches around the country, and grip-and-grin photo ops with geezers who agreed to donate to EdPAC. Locke Jones and Susan Sweetzer dumped a ton of paper on his desk every day. There was no way he could read it all, even if he was a fast reader. At the end of the day Locke Jones came in and sifted through the papers that he hadn't touched, pointing out which to sign and which to ignore. That was the boring part of the job. What was fun? Well, the golf, and those weekends at Camp David. Edsel also thought it was cool that he and Betty could screen big Hollywood movies in the White House before they were released in the movie theatres. And as boring as the public speaking was, Edsel had to admit he did get a thrill seeing himself on the evening news when he had to make those speeches.

John Edsel leaned back in his chair, hands behind his head

and feet on the desk. Maybe, he thought, he'd have fewer competitors for the job in the next election if he invited some of the likely ones for dinner and told them what it really was like. Then again, Edsel wasn't sure there would be a next election for him. He wasn't going to talk about it with anyone now, not even Betty. But three months into the Presidency, he'd pretty much decided he was going to be a one-termer. That meant, if he was going to make his mark, find his way into the history books, and make more millions for Deep-South Manufacturing, he had only forty-five months left to do it. It looked like the helicopter deal was going to happen. That was worth a cool billion dollars to Deep-South over the next couple of years. Jackson Evans, now eighty-five, had been thrilled when John Edsel gave him the news. When the deal closed, the Desert National Investment Company would pony up three billion dollars for a twenty-five percent stake in his father-in-law's company. A big chunk of that money would land in the blind trust that Edsel had set up to manage his and Betty's investments when he started his run for office.

The news media was always saying Edsel had a big advantage in that Republicans controlled both houses of Congress. The GOP could pass any law, override any filibuster. But because they had so much power, the legislators in his own party were sometimes a pain in the ass to deal with. Edsel was going nowhere on his signature move to reduce the federal deficit and send the liberals in the Northeast scurrying back into their rat holes. His advisors had done the math. Selling the state of Alaska to China would yield seven hundred billion dollars. It would get rid the country of a state that was a drain on the federal budget, sucking up more tax dollars than it produced. Finally, it would confound those left-wing Alaskan Democrats and disloyal Republicans who had combined forces to elect Levi Johnston, Sarah Palin's turncoat former son-in-law, as governor. Hell, they'd all be Chinese when John Edsel was through with them. If he managed to dump Alaska, next on his list was Hawaii. The idea of busting up the United States worried some of the old-time GOP senators, however, who kept bringing up Abraham

Lincoln and the Civil War.

"Why not sell it?" Edsel had asked them. "It if ain't working, let's fix it or get rid of it."

The GOP leadership also was worried that the Democrats were feeling so disempowered that they'd result to underhanded, possibly illegal, measures to subvert Edsel's administration. There were rumors, for example, that covert Democratic operatives had secured senior positions in key government agencies and even in the White House to spy on the President. Edsel didn't have much truck with such paranoia, but to make the party elders happy he'd deputized Jesse Grant to lead a task force to rescreen all senior staffers.

As important as his Sell Alaska initiative was, John Edsel knew capturing Abdullah bin-Salem would be the jewel in his Presidential crown. He was still getting pushback from Locke Jones and Cherry Samuels, but Edsel was adamant that he would meet with bin-Salem in the Oval Office. He wanted to awe that rag-head with the size of the place — almost thirty-six feet long by twenty-nine feet wide with a ceiling eighteen-and-a-half feet high. It was bigger than any damned tent Abdullah would ever live in. Then there was the American grandeur of it, with that fireplace on the north end and the doors opening to the Rose Garden and all that crown molding and the ceiling embossed with a medallion featuring the Presidential Seal. You weren't gonna find anything like that in all of Araby, of that Edsel was certain.

He also had decided, despite intense opposition from Locke Jones, the CIA director, and the Secret Service, that he was going to meet bin-Salem alone. The man who had succeeded Osama bin Laden as America's most-reviled enemy was going to be seated across from him, with no handcuffs constraining him. Edsel Jones didn't need bodyguards and chains to make the point that he was in charge. He was leader of the most powerful nation the world had ever seen. He was the President! In any case, if things did get out of hand, according to CIA intelligence he outweighed that Arab by a good seventy-five pounds.

Edsel still didn't know what he was going to say. Was he

going to lecture bin-Salem about the evil of his terrorist deeds? Was he going to impress upon him that America's dominance of the world was complete and impervious to any challenge, not least that of a bunch of camel jockeys? Was he going to take a stab at preaching the Gospel to this heathen? Just imagine the PR John Edsel would get if he converted Abdullah bin-Salem to Christianity, made him a Southern Baptist yet! The more Edsel thought about it, the more he realized he actually was curious about this camel-humper. Bin-Salem had come from a wealthy family. He'd had a good education. Both were things John Edsel couldn't lay claim to. So why the hell had he gone off into the desert to wage war against a country he could have sold oil to, making himself a billionaire in the process? And what was his thing about the Hollywood magazines? The CIA chief told Edsel that his men, who had raided a hotel room in Paris shortly after bin-Salem had checked out, found it littered with magazines with sexy pictures of teen girl celebrities. Now there, Edsel chuckled, was something he and that Arab had in common.

Who was this Abdullah bin-Salem? What made him tick? The more Edsel thought about it, the more he realized that was what he wanted to know. He had all the time in the world to find out. No more than five people, all with the ultimate security clearance, knew that bin-Salem was going to be a prisoner of the United States. So it's not like some damned liberal ACLU lawyer would be pounding on the front door of the White House, demanding his release. No, Edsel would figure out what this critter was all about. Then he'd pack the SOB off to Guantanamo and let him camp in another tent for the rest of his life, if he didn't just have him shot.

CHAPTER 24

SATURDAY, MARCH 21
THE FEDERAL SUITE
THE HAY-ADAMS HOTEL
WASHINGTON, DC

"We have it. Now what do we do with it?"

Good question, Jack Northern thought. He turned the tiny video camera that London had handed him over and over, marveling at how small it was. It was less than half the size of a pack of cigarettes, and yet it apparently had a chip inside that could hold three hours of video.

It was early Saturday evening, and Northern was off duty. London had invited him over for what she billed as a "planning session" with a room service dinner and an overnight stay to follow. Northern was still nervous about the idea of bugging the Oval Office. But the chance to spend another night with London Comfort? Well, there wasn't a man in America, except maybe for Locke Jones and his pals, who would turn that down.

"Who do we film? I'm not sure Bree Collard is going to be back in the Oval Office anytime soon," Northern said, recalling how upset she'd been after the last visit. "Sissy Romero? Locke Jones' assistant? She's in there with the door closed at least once a week these days."

"I'm not comfortable filming Bree unless we get her permission," London said.

"Come on!" Northern said. "We can't tell the world what we're doing London. If we're not careful, we'll both end up in jail."

"Well, is there someway maybe to position the camera so you can see it's a girl, but you can't tell that it's Bree? As far as Sissy Romero is concerned, I don't care who sees that bitch giving that dirty old man a blowjob."

London looked lost in thought for a moment.

"Jack, I've got an idea! What about filming him with me?"

"You? You've got to be kidding. You would go into the Oval Office and have sex with that man? London, I won't let that happen. That's disgusting."

"No, I wouldn't have sex with him. But I wouldn't mind him being videotaped trying to have sex with me. Just think, I could run around that big desk, with him running after me, his zipper undone and his shoes off. That would draw a big audience on E!"

Northern had to laugh. It was a hilarious image.

"Now, can you figure out a way to get it in there?"

Northern fell silent. As excited as he had been about this adventure when London first brought it up, this was put-up-or-shut-up time. Was he really going to go through with this? Was he going to destroy the reputation of the man he was supposed to protect? Was he going to run the risk of losing his job, of going to jail?

London sensed Northern's hesitation.

"Jack? I wasn't a good student. I'll admit that. I really hated history. Too many old stories about boring people and places. But since I started working with the First Lady, I've learned a lot about the White House, a lot about the President.

"She told me during one of our first tours that the Office of the President is bigger than the man who sits in it. It always will be. It symbolizes what America stands for, Jack. America doesn't stand for abusing young girls."

London reached over and held his hand, as if to seal their agreement.

"I can do it London," Northern said. "Just promise me one thing."

"What's that Jack?"

"Well, don't hurt the old man. I mean, if you knee him in the groin and hit him, there'll be hell to pay. I know they'll go after you, and me, for making that video. But if you assault him, well you damned well could get shot for that."

"Don't worry silly. I won't lay a hand on him. I'll just pretend like I'm making a movie, and when it comes time for me to go down on the old man, I'll yell 'cut' and get up and run out the door."

"So who's going to, uh, distribute this film?"

"Don't you worry. My publicist can take care of that. He doesn't give a damn about politics. But he loves anything that gets me more publicity. This sure as hell will."

Northern tucked the camera in his satchel and reached across the couch and pulled London closer.

"Whatta you say we have dessert before we order dinner?"

"I think that's a wonderful idea," London said, bouncing off the sofa and pulling him toward the bedroom.

It was ten a.m. Sunday when Northern finally left London's suite, making his way through the underground tunnel to the White House. The guards nodded hello, not bothering to ask such a familiar face for identification. They were used to visits by Jack Northern at all hours and on any day. Northern, however, was nervous. He hoped he was as good an actor as London Comfort was. He didn't want to do anything that would rouse suspicion about his dropping by the empty Oval Office on such a gloriously sunny Sunday.

Once inside the Oval Office, it took only minutes for

Northern to figure out where to plant the camera. He'd carefully cleaned it of fingerprints. Now, wearing rubber gloves, he removed a book from high on one of the shelves. He pulled the cover from the pages, cut a small hole into the spine with a penknife, and taped the camera inside. A remote control would let him start filming when he saw London enter the office. A book was a good place to hide the camera, he realized. There was little chance that John Edsel was going to open a book.

As he stepped out of the office he bumped in to Sissy Romero, which gave him a start. There were people one might expect to work weekends at the White House. Sissy Romero wasn't one of them. Her blouse was tight and one button too many was unfastened. She smiled seductively and blew him a kiss. Damn, Northern thought, is Locke Jones so gay that he doesn't even know what he's got on his hands? He smiled weakly and waved goodbye. Now he needed to head back to Arlington and dive deeply into the Black Hawk manual again. He needed to be prepped for next week's training at a secret Navy compound in Virginia. It looked as if this raid on bin-Salem was coming soon.

CHAPTER 25

THURSDAY, MARCH 26
PALESTINE STREET
JEDDAH, SAUDI ARABIA

The flight from Karachi to Jeddah is only three and a half hours. However Abdullah bin-Salem, the most famous living general in the battle against the Great Satan, couldn't just go online and book an airline ticket, even if there was an airport in the Toba Kakar Mountains. His photo was pasted in guard booths at border crossings around the world. Every airport security agent was supposed to know what he looked like. He also had the disadvantage, shared with his late mentor Osama bin Laden, of remarkable stature. A man who stood six-foot-five in his sandals would draw attention on a commercial flight, not least because he'd have trouble squeezing into even a first class seat. So most of Abdullah's journey across Pakistan was overland, by donkey, by jeep, by rusty old truck. When he reached the coast he boarded a trawler for a slower, albeit more comfortable, voyage across the Indian Ocean and through the Gulf of Aden. There his mariners shifted him into a small dhow, hoping that its lateen sail would be lost among the hundreds that fluttered across the Red Sea. They sat off the coast of Jeddah for three days, waiting for the full moon to fade. On a Wednesday night, a full five days after his departure from his windswept tent in the mountains, a combination of a waning moon and a cloudy sky offered sufficient cover for Abdullah's men to row him ashore. They deposited him on the beach at the base of Palestine Street, where, only a few hours earlier, motorbikes, horse-drawn carriages, and locals enjoying nighttime picnics had littered the sand. For the first time on this journey Abdullah was all alone. He had told the mujahideen back at the camp in Pakistan that an entourage would attract unwanted attention. They had expressed sympathy at his having to endure such a grueling journey by himself, merely to consult with the managers of Al Qaeda's account at Desert National Investment Company. "We should have online banking," joked one of them, who had worked at Citibank in New York City until the death of Osama bin Laden inspired him to return home and join the revolution. What Abdullah's men didn't know was that he could and did correspond online with Desert National any time he got close enough to Karachi to secure an Internet connection. This trip wasn't about transferring funds from one account to another or verifying that Arab National's investments on al Qaeda's behalf were Shariah-complaint. This trip was the first step in Abdullah's effort to live the life that he now knew Allah and Mohammed, peace and blessings be upon him, wanted for him.

Abdullah walked up Palestine Street, empty at four-thirty in the morning, for an early check-in at the Sofitel Jeddah Al Hamra. Thoughts of his miserable journey faded as he exulted in his solitude. There were no men watching his every move, standing outside his tent while he indulged in his Western magazines. There was no one essaying whether he should take Abdullah out and install himself in his place. Abdullah bin-Salem was free. In a matter of minutes, he had checked in and was in his room, enjoying a hot shower. He would have luxuriated in it for hours, but it was time for Fajr, the first prayer of the day. Then some sleep and a taxi to Desert National.

Later that morning, as he walked into the marble lobby of Desert National, where security guards clad in dark suits with earphones gave everyone the once over, Abdullah realized that his thawb was somewhat the worse for wear. Even with the light spritz of lemon air freshener that he'd given it in the hotel room, it gave off a beggarly smell. But that didn't seem to bother the smiling man, dressed like all the others in a black suit, who appeared suddenly at his side.

"Asalaam Alaykum," said the man, who Abdullah recognized as the president of Arab National Investment Company.

"Wa 'Alaykum Asalaam," said Abdullah, aware that he was being escorted quickly toward a private elevator to lessen the chance that anyone in the lobby would recognize him.

Once seated in the president's wood-paneled and expensively carpeted office, Abdullah explained his mission, but not before first asking the banker to offer his assurance, in Allah's name, that what he was about to learn would be kept a secret. The banker beamed with delight as he agreed. How odd, Abdullah thought, that these servants of American imperialism and the Saudi monarchy were so flattered to be asked to assist a movement dedicated to destroying it. But then he had to remember that they were investors. Abdullah had learned in university that successful investors knew how to hedge their bets against any eventuality.

The bank president listened intently and seemed nonplussed at the idea that Al Qaeda was launching an operation in Southeast Asia and needed to transfer cash to an account there that would be used to establish a physical headquarters. Yes, he could arrange a transfer of three million dollars US to Krung Thai Bank in Phuket in a matter of minutes. And, to ensure that Abdullah bin-Salem returned to his hotel without incident, the president would ask his own chauffeur to drive him from the private garage in the basement.

The men stood and bowed slightly at one another. In minutes Abdullah was in the large black limo, its tinted windows shielding him from view. As the driver headed to the Sofitel, Abdullah told him there was a change in plans. There was a tiny private airstrip on the outskirts of Jeddah where he would be meeting a friend. He wanted to be dropped there.

In thirty minutes Abdullah was boarding an aged Dassault Falcon 20. The plane's interior was worn and the exterior a bit scratched, but it was a major upgrade from days of slow sailing in antiquated trawlers. As he settled into his seat, Abdullah fondled his beard, wondering whether he'd recognize himself after he shaved it off in the jet's bathroom. Then he reached into his satchel for the flyer describing the Patong Thai Guesthouse. He was forever grateful that Allah and Mohammed, blessed be his name, were rewarding him for his service in the fight against the Great Satan by letting him devote the rest of his life to running a bed and breakfast in Phuket. His goal was to create as many Muslims as possible before he was called to Heaven.

CHAPTER 26

TUESDAY, MARCH 31
THE WEST WING, THE WHITE HOUSE
WASHINGTON, DC

"Is there something wrong with your cell phone?" Susan Sweetzer asked.

Bree looked up, embarrassed. She had been looking at her phone every ten minutes, waiting for the text that she now knew was never coming. Last night had been her third date with Randy Petty, one of the White House Fellows. It also had been the first time they had made love. London Comfort had warned her not to yield so quickly. Bree should have listened to her. What better expert, if one believed the tabloids and gossip shows, on matters of sex and romance?

"Hold out, don't put out," was the slogan London offered. "I'm serious. If you want, I'll write it on your hand."

Now, a full sixteen hours after that moment of ecstasy with Randy, Bree wished she'd taken London up on her offer. There was no response to Bree's texts to Randy suggesting a quick coffee in the White House mess. Yes, three texts had been too many, she knew that. She was looking desperate. But she was desperate. Anyway, he had said he loved her, albeit while he was on top of her, naked and rolling around on the shag carpet on her living room floor.

"Can we talk?" she texted London, who she hadn't seen since she'd transferred to Betty Edsel's office a week earlier to conduct White House tours.

"Heading to West Wing now," London texted. "I'll stop by."

Before Bree could drop her cell phone in her bag, Susan Sweetzer piped up again.

"The President. He wants to see you. In his office. Now!"

Bree hesitated. She didn't want to go.

"Now Bree!" Sweetzer commanded.

Bree grimaced and stood up. She had rehearsed in her mind how she would handle another move by John Edsel, but she was feeling so vulnerable now she wasn't sure she could stand up to him. The ten-foot walk to the Oval Office door seemed to take hours. Was this, Bree wondered, what prisoners on death row felt like as they marched to the gas chamber? Why was it that John Edsel was the only man who wanted to see her again? Was a quick blowjob all a man would ever want from her?

"Come right on in, young lady," John Edsel bellowed. Bree stepped into the Oval Office, and the Marine standing in for Jack Northern pulled the door closed behind her.

London Comfort could hear the soft but heavy sound of the door closing as she stepped into the anteroom that Susan Sweetzer and Bree Collard shared.

"Where's Bree?" she asked.

"She's with the President," Sweetzer said, looking annoyed at being questioned by an underling. "I'd suggest you girls gossip at lunch time. There's work to do."

London's initial impulse was to rush past Sweetzer and fling open the door to the President's office, not a wise move she knew, given the presence of a Marine guard, the possibility that the door was locked on the inside, and her likely re-imprisonment at the Central Regional Detention Facility in LA once she'd been wrestled to the floor and handcuffed. Then she remembered another option.

"Yes ma'am," she said to Sweetzer so deferentially that the President's secretary looked up from her desk, astonished.

London dug into her purse and found the remote control to the video camera installed in the President's office, which Jack Northern had left with her went he left on some sort of training exercise. London clicked the button that read "start."

Minutes later, as London walked back toward the East Wing, a hysterical Bree Collard rushed past her, sobbing so loudly that various Presidential advisors opened their doors to see what was going on. Then Locke Jones raced by from the other direction, almost shoving London out of the way. Susan Sweetzer looked on in amazement.

###

When Locke Jones walked into the President's office, he noticed that John Edsel's face was more flushed than usual.

"Locke, we got a problem. I need your help. This Bree, we gotta get rid of her. The girl comes on to me every time I bring her into this office. She practically tries to rape me. She tells me she wants to be my wife. I mean she's a damn little girl, and, frankly, she's a piece of trash. She just went crazy on me Locke. She tried to hit me! I want you to get rid of her. I don't want to know about it. Just do it."

"Mr. President," Locke interjected.

"No ifs, ands, or buts Locke. That is a Presidential order."

"Yes sir, Mr. President. I'll take care of it," Jones said.

Locke walked back to his office and collapsed into his chair. He was facing what, in Alabama, they called a "come to Jesus" moment. Was he really going to protect this rapacious, homophobic, sexist moron who preyed on young women? Was he going to "get rid of" Bree Collard? If he was, what was he expected to do? Kill her? How the hell could Locke Jones keep a crazy young girl from going public about John Edsel's deviant behavior? Was Edsel's father-in-law going to have to shell out the cash for another mansion in Alabama, like he'd done to buy the silence of one of Edsel's female assistants in Montgomery? Whatever Locke Jones decided to do would dictate the direction of his career, his life, as much as it would that of John Edsel. Maybe he thought, it was time to be himself, although he now realized he had lost touch with what that self might be. Gay, that was part of it. But what else? Was he a conservative Republican? Not really. His was a job, it wasn't a calling. It wasn't something he felt passionate about, something he believed in. Locke Jones didn't really know what he believed in beyond Gucci, and sometimes Prada. He felt ashamed of himself.

Locke had often thought how proud his father, an investment banker from Boston, would have been had he lived long enough to see his son working in the White House. His father's pride. He realized that was a big part of his motivation for taking this job and sticking with it. Stanley Jones was long dead though, and the time for earning his pride was long gone. Now, Locke realized, the only pride that mattered was his own. On the other hand, there was the matter of ending a career with real financial promise. He wasn't making much money as a government employee. But people like him worked in government mostly to prep themselves for more lucrative corporate work. That, Locke was sure, was only a year or two away.

There were other gay conservative Republicans who had converted and done okay, and without the help of Michelle Bachman's husband, thank you. Take David Brock, for example, who came out as gay and switched from Right to Left after his failure to turn up damaging information about Hillary Clinton kept his book about her from becoming a best seller. Then there was Ken Mehlman, manager of George W. Bush's 2004 re-election campaign, who remained a Republican after he came out as gay but began lobbying for gay marriage.

The phone rang, interrupting Locke's rare moment of self-examination. Sissy Romero asked if he would take a call from Jackson Evans. But of course.

"Locke Jones. It's Jackson Evans. How are you young man?"

"It's good to hear from you Mr. Evans. I'm doing fine.

Things are going quite well here."

"Well now, that's not what I hear. Just got off the phone with the President. Seems he's gotten himself in another one of those damned situations Locke. I want to help you fix it."

"Fix it, sir?"

"You know what I mean Locke. My damned son-in-law can't keep it in his pants. If this gets out, there's hell to pay. The Kudzu deal is dead, for one thing. The John Edsel presidency might not have much life left to it either. If Betty finds out, it will destroy her."

So Betty Edsel didn't know about her husband's philandering and her father did? Locke guessed blood wasn't thicker than water when money and power and influence were involved.

"What do we do Mr. Evans?"

"I'm flying up to DC tonight so we can talk about that Locke. This ain't something I want to talk about on the phone. Also Locke, I want to talk about an opportunity for you. Mid-South is needing someone to run its lobbying in DC. Damn good job for a guy like you. Pays about four times what John says they're paying you now. He moaned and groaned, but I told him I want you. You help me keep this mess quiet Locke, and that job is yours, you hear?"

"Yes sir Mr. Evans. Give me a ring when you land. I'm available whenever you are. Maybe an early breakfast tomorrow?"

Locke hung up the phone. A salary four times what he was making now? Locke looked at the lining of his Gucci jacket, which was a bit frayed. He'd had this particular pair of shoes re-stitched twice. Could he afford to postpone being himself for a few more years? Could he afford not to?

CHAPTER 27

FRIDAY, APRIL 2
THE WEST WING, THE WHITE HOUSE
WASHINGTON, DC

Not showing up for work one day was bad enough. Not showing up the next day either, and not bothering to call in? The damned girl wasn't even answering her phone. Susan Sweetzer was beside herself.

She fired off an email, her preferred method of communication with those she didn't want to talk to.

"London, come to my office please."

With no White House tour scheduled, London headed to the West Wing. When she got to Susan Sweetzer's office she noticed that Bree wasn't at her desk.

"London, your friend Bree Collard hasn't seen fit to show up for work for two days now. She hasn't even had the decency to call and explain herself. Do you know what's going on?"

"No, ma'am. I don't have any idea."

"You haven't talked to her? She hasn't been texting you?"

"I told you no. I have no idea."

"Well, I'd like you to run over to her apartment and see what's going on. You tell her that if she doesn't get her sweet ass into this office by noon today, she is out of a job. Understand?"

London nodded yes.

London was worried about Bree. She'd called her several times since the incident in Edsel Jones' office, but Bree never answered. As worried as she was, London wasn't sure she was up for doing therapy. She needed some of her own. Jason had called the night before, begging to see her, and not-so-subtly threatening that his video of him and London having sex was going to go viral if she didn't. The call had enraged London. But she wasn't so much mad at Jason as at herself. How had she ever let herself get involved with such a person? London Comfort, the dumb slut, was supposed to have been a role she was playing. She'd let it become her life. When Jason hung up, London's first thought was to call Jack Northern. He would listen, he would understand, he would know what to do. But Jack Northern was nowhere, or at least nowhere that she could find him. He was off on a training mission. He told her it was Top Secret, and he couldn't say anything more, including exactly when he'd be back.

London took her cell phone from her Birkin and texted Kameela that she was on her way. She was on a mission, and she needed company. In ten minutes she was back at her suite at the Hay-Adams. Kameela was ready to roll. She already had called a taxi and headed downstairs to find a way for London to get into it without being assailed by the paparazzi.

The traffic was miserable, and it took almost fifteen minutes to get to Bree Collard's apartment building. London had never been there. Susan Sweetzer had the address though and, what London thought odd, the password for entry to her building. London called from the sidewalk first, getting only Bree's voicemail. Then she buzzed Bree's apartment from the building's front door. No answer. So she and Kameela walked in and took the elevator to the third floor, Apt. 307.

They knocked and waited, knocked and waited. Clearly Bree Collard wasn't at home. Had she run away? Had she decided to go back to her mother in Raleigh and get away from it all?

London hoped so. Life in John Edsel's White House was difficult, especially for someone as fragile as Bree Collard.

"She's not here. Let's go," she said to Kameela and turned to head for the elevator.

"Just a minute London," Kameela said. She tried the knob to Bree's apartment door. It was unlocked.

"My God," London said. "That's so strange. Why would she run away and leave the door unlocked?"

"You forget I worked for the police department, London," Kameela said. "This may be stranger than you think."

The two of them stepped quietly into Bree's living room, shabby with its orange shag rug and cheap beige sofa. The tiny kitchen sink was stacked with dishes. Blouses and pants and dresses were draped over the back of the couch and two living room chairs. London called Bree's name again. No answer. Then Kameela pushed open the door to Bree's bedroom. The curtains were drawn on this cloudy Washington morning, and all either could see was a mound of blankets and pillows. Then London spotted a pale and slender foot protruding from underneath.

Kameela pulled back the blankets. The Bree Collard before them looked more peaceful than she ever had in the few weeks London had known her. She seemed to have a smile on her face.

"She's dead, London," Kameela said, feeling Bree's slender wrist for a pulse. "She's dead."

Kameela looked around the bed and spotted an empty plastic pill bottle on the nightstand. While London dialed 911, Kameela quickly tucked the container in her burka. London sat on the edge of the bed and stroked Bree's hair. Five minutes later, time when neither Kameela nor London spoke, the police were at the apartment door.

Both Kameela and London were taken downtown to police headquarters for questioning. In less than an hour they were released, thanks to a call from Susan Sweetzer, who vouched that she had sent London to Bree Collard's apartment to investigate her failure to appear for work. There would be a coroner's examination, a detective told London. The best guess at this point was suicide.

###

London didn't return to work. Betty Edsel was understanding when London called and told her what she'd experienced, inviting her to stop by the family quarters if she needed to talk about what she was feeling. London marveled at how much that woman acted like a mother, and she meant that in a good way. London declined the First Lady's offer. Instead she and Kameela headed back to the Hay-Adams. London took an Ativan and crawled into bed. Kameela excused herself to run an errand.

Back on the street, Kameela hailed a taxi for a trip to Eustice Pharmacy in Adams Morgan. She walked up to the prescription counter and presented the brown plastic container that she'd taken from Bree's nightstand.

"I'd like a refill of my Klonopin," she told the pharmacist.

"Can you give me your date of birth, ma'am?"

"August 8, 1991," Kameela replied, an obvious lie to anyone willing to look Kameela, age forty, in the face. The pharmacist, however, merely went to her computer to check the refill status.

"Ma'am, there's something odd about this prescription. It wasn't filled here."

"But it says Eustice Pharmacy on the label. And that's my name, Bree Collard."

"I'm sorry Miss Collard, but you aren't in our database. There's some kind of mistake here."

Kameela snatched the bottle from the woman's hand.

"All right then," she snarled. "I'll get my refill at CVS."

###

It was eight p.m. when London awoke from her Ativan-induced sleep. She was hungry. It took her a few seconds to recall the horrors of that afternoon, which seemed like a distant nightmare. Kameela was in the sitting room, tapping away at London's laptop.

"London, there's something suspicious here," Kameela said

when London walked into the room. "Look at this."

London looked at the brown plastic bottle in Kameela's hand. A thirty-day supply of Klonopin, four milligrams a day, from Eustice Pharmacy, dated April 1. The bottle was empty.

"Where did you get this, Kameela? You didn't take it from Bree's bedroom?"

"That exactly where I got it."

"But this is probably what she used to kill herself. You should have given it to the police."

"Yes, and the police would have decided exactly that. Suicide. Case closed. Given what you told me about Bree's hysterics and that crazy President, I decided to check this out. This drug store didn't fill this prescription, London. This drug store doesn't have Bree Collard's name in its computer. Someone faked this label. I'll bet Bree Collard died of an overdose of Klonopin. I'll also bet she didn't swallow it on her own."

"Oh my God! Kameela, do you think someone killed her?"

"What really went on in that Oval Office, London? We've got to find out."

"Well we can find out Kameela. We have it on tape. The problem is Jack Northern isn't here to get that tape. I know where it is. I just don't know how to lay my hands on it. Unless... unless I go into his office and just see if I can get it. I mean, why not?"

"You be careful young lady. I don't want to see you back in prison in LA, this time without me there to watch out for you."

London smiled.

"Don't worry Kameela. I can pull this off. Tomorrow night let's make sure we order some popcorn from room service. We're going to have some movies to watch. But I gotta warn you, it won't be pretty."

Henry E. Scott

CHAPTER 28

FRIDAY, APRIL 3
THE OVAL OFFICE, THE WHITE HOUSE
WASHINGTON, DC

London approached the door to the Oval Office, giving the Marine guard her most seductive smile. He reached for the door to open it.

"Just a minute, young lady. Where do you think you're going? The President isn't in there just now."

"Don't worry Miss Sweetzer," London said. "I'm just delivering some papers. The President asked me to deliver them myself and put them right in the middle of his desk."

Sweetzer looked on, clearly suspicious, as the guard opened the door, and London Comfort walked into the empty Oval Office. Once inside, London marveled again at the decor. She wished she could take the time to appreciate it, but the President might come back at any moment. London knew she had to move fast.

She scanned the bookcase, spotting the place where Jack Northern had secreted the video camera. The hole in the spine of that book looked so obvious, but she guessed that was only the case if you knew what you were looking for. London kicked off her shoes and pushed a chair toward the place where the book was shelved. As she reached up to grab the book where the camera was concealed, she felt a sweaty hand on the bare calf of her right leg.

"Well, young lady, it's nice to see you taking an interest in America history," said John Edsel, sliding his hand slowly up and down London Comfort's leg.

"Oh my God," London said as she slipped off the chair, almost collapsing on the floor.

"Mr. President. I'm sorry," she said as she picked herself up. "I was dropping off some papers, and I was just so impressed by how many books you have in here."

London was terrified, and she knew the President could see right through her. But there was no escaping now. She pushed "start" on the video camera remote control that dangled like a charm from her bracelet.

"Well, I'd be happy to give you a grand tour some time. I've been thinking we need to get to know one another a bit better."

Edsel stood so close to London that she could feel his breath on her face as he talked. He reached his right arm out and wrapped it around her shoulder, pulling her closer to him. Then his left arm dropped, and his hand was on her butt.

"Maybe you could entertain me with some stories about your life in Hollywood. That sounds like quite a swinging town."

At that Edsel stepped even closer. London could see the bulge of his erection. She struggled to slip away from him.

"Whassa matter? Now don't tell me I'm too old for you. You know, age is all in your head. And you can see I'm feeling damned young when I'm around you."

"Mr. President, please," London said. "I don't think this is appropriate."

"What's not appropriate, Ms. Comfort? I mean, it ain't like I don't know what you been doing in Hollywood. I read those gossip magazines. I watch those TV shows. 'Secret sex film shows London Comfort fit to be tied.' Isn't that what US Weekly is saying this week? So how about getting comfortable with John Edsel? How about performing for your Commander in Chief?"

Edsel slid his left hand up and under London's blouse and cupped her right breast. He planted his lips on hers, his tongue pushing hard against her firmly clenched teeth. London struggled to get free, twisting and pushing. His grip tightened. His lips pressed so firmly on hers that she thought he might damage her teeth.

London relaxed her mouth and John Edsel pushed his tongue inside. Then she bit down hard until the old man screamed. She stepped back and saw a froth of blood and spit on his lips.

"You goddamned bitch," he sputtered, his Southern diction made worse by his swelling tongue. "I'm gonna put your ass back in that jail."

John Edsel rushed into his bathroom, slamming the door behind him. London stepped back on the chair, pulling the tiny video camera from its hiding place. She grabbed her shoes and darted barefoot out the door past Susan Sweetzer, who looked puzzled but not especially alarmed at the commotion and the faint noise emanating from the Oval Office. There was no time to waste. London ran back to her desk and grabbed her bag. In a matter of minutes she had raced through the underground passageway and back to the Hay-Adams. She handed the camera to Kameela and told her to hide it in her room in case the Secret Service was on its way to search London's.

The Secret Service never came. But an hour later Roberto Diaz was on the telephone.

"London, what the hell did you do? They want to send you back to prison in LA. They say you assaulted the President of the United States."

"Who says, Roberto? Did you talk to that dirty old man?"

"No, I talked to Locke Jones, my friend. He's freaking out. They say you bit the President. He was bleeding. London, you could go to jail for years for something like this."

"Roberto, I want you to get your ass to DC right now. Take the next flight out. This isn't what you think it is. It's a helluva lot bigger than you think it is. There's more publicity in what I've got to tell you, what I've got to show you, than you've seen in your whole damned career."

###

At seven p.m. room service brought up a large bowl of popcorn and an ice bucket filled with soft drinks. Kameela and London sat on the sofa, London's laptop perched on the seat of a chair in front of them, to watch the first of a series of video clips that Kameela had transferred to a flash drive. London had warned Kameela that the content might be graphic. Kameela had assured her that there wasn't anything she'd see in these videos that hadn't she seen or done in the old days in South Central LA.

The first clip was Sissy Romero. There wasn't any coercion involved.

"That damned slut," London said, watching as Romero ripped open her blouse and hiked her skirt before John Edsel could even lay a hand on her.

It was the next clip that alarmed them. Bree Collard, on her knees, was crying uncontrollably. John Edsel, his zipper undone, has pushing her face toward his crotch. Suddenly Bree hit him in groin and ran from the Oval Office. As bad as that was, it wasn't nearly as alarming as what followed. London and Comfort watched as President Edsel called in Locke Jones and ordered him to get rid of Bree Collard. Now, three days later, Bree Collard was dead.

The final episode, which featured London struggling against John Edsel's ever tightening embrace, seemed almost funny. Kameela laughed when she saw the President spewing spit and blood as he screamed at London. Then they both fell silent.

"London, you saw what happened to Bree Collard," Kameela said. "Girl, we are in danger. Tonight I'm going to be sleeping on this sofa and not in my room down the hall"

Kameela pulled from her burka a Smith & Wesson pistol and laid it on the coffee table. London was amazed, both at the pistol and the fact that Kameela's burka seemed to conceal so many surprises.

"I'll be back in a few minutes," Kameela said. "If something happens, I need to make sure we have some bargaining power."

"Bargaining power? Bargaining with who, with what?"

"I want you to trust me London. I want to put a copy of this video in the hands of a friend of mine. If something happens to us, he'll make sure it gets out. If we get arrested, we just need to let President John Edsel know there's a copy floating out there that will come to light if we aren't freed."

London was frightened. Suddenly she felt as if she were living one of those spy movies Justin used to love. Kameela headed for the lobby to leave a copy of the video in an envelope with Ahmed Azhar's name on it. Inside she tucked a note reminding him of their deal — the tape of John Edsel in exchange for the tape of Justin and London Comfort. No sooner had Kameela returned to London's suite than the telephone rang. It was the White House. London wasn't sure whether she should take the call.

"Hello?"

"This is the First Lady's office calling for London Comfort," said the voice on the other end.

The First Lady? Could it be that she knew what had happened? Was she angry at London? London wanted to bring down the President of the United States. Now she realized that she might hurt Betty Edsel in doing it.

"Yes ma'am. This is London Comfort."

The First Lady immediately was on the line.

"London, you are in serious danger. I want you and your escort to grab some clothes and take the tunnel back to the White House. My secretary will meet you there. Then we've got to get you out of here. And London, don't answer any more phone calls. Don't answer any knocks on your door. This is very serious young lady. I'll see you in five minutes."

"Can we trust her?" Kameela asked. "After all, she's his wife. If he goes down, what happens to her?"

It was a good question. London's gut told her the answer was "yes."

"Let's pack. Quickly. We need to be at the White House in

five minutes. And Kameela, bring that gun."

Exactly five minutes later, London and Kameela, carrying a single bag in which they'd packed some toiletries and a change of clothes, stood at the White House door of the Hay-Adams tunnel. Now, London realized, she'd know if the concern Betty Edsel had shown was real.

Lydia Crinkle greeted London and Kameela as they walked into the White House basement and whisked them by various guards. In minutes they were stepping outside the East Wing, where a large black limousine with tinted windows was waiting, its engines running. The driver opened the door. Inside was a very upset Betty Edsel.

"Get in. Get in. We don't have much time."

As the driver sped off, Betty Edsel pressed a button to raise the soundproof barrier between his seat and theirs.

"I know everything now. London, I am so sorry this has happened to you. I am so sorry this has happened to Bree Collard. I hope you can forgive me. I had my suspicions. But if I'd known things like this were happening, well, I would have stopped it. Now we have to get you girls to a safe place."

"I have an idea ma'am," Kameela said. "I know a motel where we can stay. A place they'd never expect to find us. If your driver can leave us somewhere in Shaw, we can hail a taxi and go there. It would look very suspicious to have a car like this deliver us."

"Absolutely," Betty Edsel said. "And don't worry. You're going to be all right. I'm going to see to that. I have things to take care of on my end. Just be careful. No long cell phone calls — they can trace those. Maybe change your hotel from time to time. And text me every day, okay? I want to know you're safe."

CHAPTER 29

FRIDAY, APRIL 3
COLUMBIA HOTEL
RHODE ISLAND AVENUE NW
WASHINGTON, DC

Exhausted from the stress of their flight from the Hay-Adams, London Comfort and Kameela Ishaad collapsed on their beds. London wondered if she wouldn't sleep better on the floor than on the bed in his miserable motel room. As she shifted her body in an effort to get comfortable, she felt something like metal springs through the thin mattress underneath her. The bedspread was made of some sort of plastic thread, with a pattern that reminded London of what she'd seen the first, and only, time she'd dropped acid. Making matters worse, if that was possible, was the smell. London had the distinct impression that other occupants hadn't bothered to go to the toilet when they needed to urinate.

"Pretty shabby, huh?" Kameela said from her own bed, a few feet away.

"Yeah. I don't know how they can call something like this a

bed. I'd rather be in a hammock or lying on the floor. And that smell! It stinks in here."

"Welcome to my world London, or at least what used to be my world. I can't tell you how many nights I've spent in dumps like this. But it's cheap, and those damned photographers aren't likely to be hanging around outside."

"I bet they don't have room service?" London asked. "I'm hungry."

"Room service. The only room service they have in a place like this is for horny old men looking for young girls. If you want food, you got to go to those vending machines in the lobby and buy a pack of crackers and a cola."

"Oh my God, can't we do better than that?"

"Well, there are some restaurants around here that we could go it. I can introduce you to a little soul food," Kameela said, smiling. "I'm not going to be able to eat halal, but Allah will forgive me under the circumstances. And you aren't going to be able to go dressed like that."

A few minutes later, London and Kameela walked out the door of their dingy room, dressed in matching burkas. Kameela had worked wonders with a few safety pins from her toiletry bag, although it was clear to any careful observer that London Comfort wasn't wearing a burka custom-made for her. Still, it was an effective disguise, although a bit scratchy. London's bright blue eyes were the only thing left uncovered.

They walked several blocks down streets that London hadn't imagined existed. There was trash on the sidewalk and in the gutter. Florescent lights blinked in the windows of those shops that were open; others were covered by steel grates. There were men standing, sitting, even laying on the sidewalk, some covered with pieces of cardboard that gave London a better appreciation for her motel quilt. Yet, there were glimpses of happiness on these dark and oppressive and dangerous streets. Little boys and girls giggled as their mothers, who tugging them along the sidewalks, smiled back in return. A man and woman walked hand in hand down the sidewalk, stopping at a corner for a goodbye kiss as they parted. London watched as the man turned half a block away to look again at the woman he'd just left behind. Already he was missing her. The occasional woman even smiled at both Kameela and London, who seemed, in their burkas, to be invisible to the men on the street. What could these people be happy about, London wondered? Then again, what had she been happy about, living in a world that was the antithesis of this? She had had everything a girl could want — a beautiful home, stylish clothes, expensive vacations, a gorgeous car. However, she hadn't had a mother who smiled at her. She hadn't had anyone who held her hand as she walked down a street except for Mariel, who was paid to do it. Given that he was never home, London even had had to take her father's love as a matter of faith.

The last few weeks in Washington had been an education in politics. But London realized that the most valuable lesson she'd learned was that there was much more to life then you could fit into a Bentley or a Vuitton trunk. If only Jack were here to hold her hand and walk down these streets with her. While she had loved her time with him — the sex, the cuddling, the conversation — she loved him even more now that he was away. Not knowing where he was, or when she would see him again, was difficult. For a second, London felt an odd little pain in her chest. Was this what they called heartache?

The meal at the Dew Drop Diner was an experience. Never before had London ingested so much fat. Fried chicken. Collards larded with bits of pork. Strange pieces of bread that Kameela called "hush puppies." By the time they got back to the motel, the food was weighing heavily on London. She felt like she was pregnant. No sooner did Kameela enter the room than she washed her hands and forearms and face three times and rinsed her mouth. It was time, she told London, for Isha, the last prayer of the day. She unrolled her prayer rug and stood to say "Allahu akbar." Still in her burka, London stood by Kameela's side, marveling at the complex ritual. While she couldn't recite the obligatory prayers, she found herself mimicking Kameela's bow toward the Kaaba, her forward prostration, and finally her rotation backwards to a sitting position. The words of the prayer rolled over her and through her and, despite the day's dangers and her longing for Jack, London felt at peace with herself.

CHAPTER 30

TUESDAY, APRIL 7
SOMEWHERE IN THE AIR OVER PAKISTAN

Jack Northern looked at his watch. He already was an hour into what he'd been told would be a two-hour flight from Kandahar to Abdullah bin-Salem's isolated encampment in Pakistan's Toba Kakar Mountains. Back in the United States, by this time he'd already have landed at Camp David and escorted John Edsel to the main lodge at the President's weekend retreat. This was far from the sort of weekend getaway that occasioned most of Jack Northern's helicopter trips.

Save for the constant drone of the engines, it was eerily quiet. Northern was on the lead copter, each of which carried twelve men. His team would land first and secure the perimeter around the bin-Salem encampment while, a minute later, the second copter would land and discharge the team that had been commanded by President Edsel himself to bring bin-Salem back alive. Northern looked around him. The men looked bored. He didn't see any signs of the anxiety that he felt, despite his weeks of training with these guys at a simulated camp in the Virginia mountains. There was the occasional yawn. The occasional glance at a watch. The weary looks of men who just wanted to get this job over with and get back home.

Northern tried unsuccessfully to stretch his long body in the tight space to which he was confined. He smiled. Sitting on this copter, the Defense Department's newly acquired Kudzu 990, he wasn't responsible for defending a morally corrupt President, a man whose venality and stupidity appalled him. He wasn't struggling, as he had in recent weeks, with whether it was right to conspire with London to force Edsel from office. He was actually risking his life to protect his nation from the most dangerous man on the face of the earth. He'd never been more proud of himself.

It was one p.m. when Locke Jones walked into the Situation Room in the White House basement. On the opposite wall were four flat-panel video monitors that showed barely visible images captured by drones of the pitch-black Toba Kakar Mountains, where it was two o'clock in the next day's morning. Another two screens showed the barely lit interiors of two Kudzu 990 helicopters, each packed tight with a dozen Navy SEALS and one with the additional presence of Jack Northern.

Jones surveyed the group President Edsel had invited to watch this momentous expedition. He had expected Defense Secretary Samuels, Joint Chiefs of Staff Chairman Ludlow, Navy Secretary Roster, the Director for Counterterrorism, the Assistant Commanding General for the Joint Special Operations Command, and the National Security Advisor, although the size of the group made him wonder if Ron Paul's 2011 campaign for smaller government hadn't been a good idea after all. What shocked him was the presence of Vice President Jesse Grant, who he didn't trust any farther than he could throw him, an expressions Jones had learned in his campaign work down South. Jones pulled Samuels aside.

"What's he doing in here?" he asked, pointing at Grant.

Samuels shrugged. "The President invited him."

John Edsel was in a great mood, laughing and slapping Grant and General Ludlow on the back. Someone had placed a tray of tiny barbecue sandwiches in front of him, something that definitely was not on his new diet, and Edsel was washing them down with a can of RC Cola.

Through Edsel's guffaws Locke could hear the running commentary of the intelligence staffers who were closely observing the drone video feeds and gathering other information about what might be happening on the ground. Their best guess was that Kudzu One and Kudzu Two, as they labeled them, were ten minutes away from Abdullah bin-Salem's camp.

Edsel slapped his hand on the table to get the attention of his subordinates. He asked each of them to take an RC Cola and stand.

"Ladies and gentlemen, I'd like to propose a toast to the brave men on those two copters who are risking their lives to capture this terrorist son of a bitch. I'd also like to thank all of you have had a hand in making this possible. Ladies and gentlemen, God Bless America!"

With that the officials around the table took quick slugs of the national beverage of what once had been the Confederate States of America. Locke was amused to see a couple of them grimace at the taste.

No sooner had they sat back down than images began appearing on the formerly dark video monitors. In quick succession: A cluster of some thirty tents, what looked to be a flash from a rifle, a huge tarp, probably a tent, sucked up from the ground and into the air, then the blade of Kudzu One sailing up and off its mounting to slice through Kudzu Two. In seconds both helicopters crashed to the ground, bursting into flames. The intelligence team calmly narrated what was happening. The Mission Room audience sat stunned and silent.

"Oh my God," said Cherry Samuels, the first to speak. She burst into tears.

"What the hell happened?" Edsel asked.

"Listen," interrupted General Ludlow. "They're saying the

damned blade broke off that chopper."

Ludlow and Roster exchanged quick and angry looks.

"Madame Secretary, this was what we warned you about," Ludlow said, evidently unconcerned that this public upbraiding of the Defense Secretary would cost him his job.

The room emptied in minutes, with Roster and Ludlow, huddled together as they walked out the door, the only ones talking. Locke Jones headed for the bathroom on the second floor. He felt like he would throw up. He'd lost a friend, albeit a casual one, in Jack Northern. He'd lost a reputation as the Special Advisor to this President, whose personal ties to the Kudzu manufacturer were sure to surface in the ensuing investigation. Those twelve SEALS, men who Locke Jones had met, whose hands he had shaken — they were dead. He took off his jacket, loosened his tie, and splashed some cold water on his face. Then he headed to the Oval Office for some crisis planning.

For once, John Edsel wasn't sprawled in his chair, jacketless, with his feet on the desk. He almost looked small, sitting like a penitent in the chair behind the desk, his head bowed and staring at his hands. He looked up as Jones approached.

"What do we do now, Locke?" he asked. "What do we do now?"

There was no easy way out of this, Locke Jones knew. He needed to schedule a quick press conference for later in the afternoon, and he'd spend the next few hours developing a spin. For one thing, there was no way the President would accept that the problem had been with the Kudzu. They'd name a panel, a panel very friendly to John Edsel, to investigate thoroughly what appeared to be a mechanical failure but may have been an attack from the ground. That would take a good year, Locke estimated. Plenty of time to refurbish John Edsel's badly tarnished reputation.

At four p.m. the President's press secretary, Jack Sousa, stepped up to the rostrum in the White House Press Room. A couple of dozen reporters sat and stood in front of him. The word was that this conference would be about a disaster. Exactly how big a disaster, what kind of a disaster, no one knew.

Sousa introduced John Edsel, who stepped to the podium, blinking as his eyes adjusted to the rapid flashes of the news photographers. He made a brief announcement: There had been a crash of two Navy helicopters over a mountain pass in Pakistan. Two dozen Navy SEALS had perished. There would be a thorough investigation into the cause of the crash. He would take no more questions. Loud questions filled the room as Locke Jones escorted the President out the door. Sousa stayed behind to repeat, firmly and repeatedly, that there was no more to say.

Only two hours later, as the six o'clock news anchors took their seats and their cameras went live, it was clear that Locke Jones' strategy wasn't working. The air was rife with rumor. It had been an effort to kill Abdullah bin-Salem. Pakistan was outraged, again, at U.S. trespass on its territory. The problem had been the helicopters, newly purchased by the Defense Department against the advice of its analysts. The manufacturer of the helicopters was John Edsel's father-in-law. John Edsel's father-in-law had filed with the SEC a notice of a proposed major investment by the Arab National Investment Company. An Arab company owning a stake in the US manufacturer of a helicopter that failed in a mission to capture an Arab terrorist? What, the reporters were asking, was that all about?

Locke Jones sat in his office with his elbows on his desk and his head in his hands. He was good, but he wasn't good enough to paper over this. The whole country would be calling for John Edsel's resignation. Already the chairman of the Republican Party, who had recruited John Edsel, was saying on Fox News that the President had to go. Jones would be out of a job. And his career as Mid-South's chief lobbyist? Mid-South would be lucky if it was still in business after the investigation was over. Locke Jones would be lucky if he wasn't forced to trade his worn Gucci jackets for the orange jumpsuits they still wore on prison work gangs.

Jones looked up when his cell phone buzzed to announce a text message. Anderson Cooper was tweeting that there were videos on the web of John Edsel having sex in the Oval Office.

Jones hurled the cell phone across the room, smashing it into the wall. Then, his curiosity trumping his anger, he logged onto his computer. Sissy Romero, Bree Collard, London Comfort! Someone was raising a question about Bree Collard's death. Jesus Christ, John Edsel probably would be wearing his own orange jumpsuit soon. Jones just hoped they didn't end up being cellmates.

His phone rang. A shaken Susan Sweetzer was summoning him to the President's office. The two-minute stroll was the longest walk of Locke Jones' life.

"Well, Locke, what do we do?" John Edsel asked.

"Mr. President, I think you know the answer to that," Jones responded.

"I do Locke. I do. I want you to write my resignation speech. Let's keep it brief."

At six thirty p.m., a single news pool television camera was turned on in the Oval Office. A tired and dejected John Edsel announced his resignation. Locke Jones sat in his office, scanning the four television monitors. Before the commentators could begin opining about what had just happened, the networks broke through with word of another major story. As Jones watched from his desk, every television network in the nation showed Jesse Grant walking into the White House pressroom and stepping onto the podium to face the Chief Justice of the Supreme Court. Jesse Grant was sworn in as the forty-seventh President of the United States of America. Betty Edsel was beside him, holding the Bible.

CHAPTER 31

TUESDAY, APRIL 7
COLUMBIA HOTEL
RHODE ISLAND AVENUE NW
WASHINGTON, DC

The flight from Karachi to Jeddah is only three and a half London Comfort's cell phone rang. The White House. She wondered whether she should answer. She remembered that Betty Edsel had said to keep any calls brief so they couldn't be traced.

"This is the White House. The First Lady is calling for London Comfort," said the voice on the other end of the line. London took the call.

"London, this is Betty Edsel. Are you okay? Have you seen the news?"

Seen the news? The rabbit-eared television set was one of many things that didn't work in the miserable motel room that London and Kameela Ishaad had called home for the past few days.

"No ma'am," she said.

"You're safe London. Something has happened, but you are safe. I am sending a car for you and your friend. Let me know where you are, and my driver will pick you up and bring you to the White House. Then I can explain everything."

London turned to Kameela, who looked worried, and smiled.

"It's all over," she said. "Let's pack up. We're getting out of here."

Betty Edsel had sent the limo for London Comfort. Now she had to decide how to help herself. She picked up her phone and asked her driver to take her to her father's hotel.

When she walked into Jackson Evans' suite half an hour later, the old man was sitting in his wheelchair, his eyes red. Betty had never known her father to cry.

"Darling, I am so sorry," he said. "I am so sorry. I never meant for this to turn out this way."

"What are you talking about Daddy?" Betty said. "Are you talking about the helicopters, or the girls? You knew about them too, didn't you?"

Jackson Evans lowered his head toward his lap, and Betty had her answer. She was no fool. She'd heard the rumors, and she'd decided to protect herself by not digging for the truth. But she couldn't believe that her father had known too and hadn't told her. Now they no longer were merely rumors. She couldn't overlook them. She'd be damned if she would be another Hillary Clinton.

She also was upset by the other allegations. The John Edsel she knew would never have authorized the murder of Bree Collard. Then again, did she really know John Edsel? Getting the Defense Department to buy those shoddy helicopters from her father's company? That was less surprising, but upsetting nonetheless.

"Daddy, you remember John Northern, that young Secret Service agent who guarded John? I called his parents today to tell them how sorry I was that he died in that helicopter crash. It broke my heart to hear his mother cry. Can you imagine how the parents of those other young Navy SEALS are feeling?"

"I'm going to do all I can to make this right by you," Jackson Evans said. "I know I can't undo this. But I'm going to see that son of a bitch gets what he deserves.

"And those young men that died? Betty, I wish I'd been in the helicopter with them. I can't bring them back to life, but maybe I can join them."

Betty Edsel walked out of the room, leaving her father in his wheelchair, convulsed with sobs. When she got back to her East Wing office, London Comfort and Kameela Ishaad were waiting. She finally had some good news to deliver — neither was in danger any more. She sat them on the sofa and began to recount the events of the past few days.

London was surprised that the First Lady could tell the story of her husband's betrayal without showing any anger. Her manner, starting out, was as matter of fact as when she gave London her first White House tour. She hesitated, however, before she mentioned London's appearance on the leaked video.

"My dear, I'm so sorry that happened to you. I am sorry, and I am ashamed."

"Ma'am, there is no need to apologize. It wasn't your fault," London said, now realizing that Betty Edsel had no idea of her role in setting up the video sting.

Then the First Lady told London and Kameela about the death of the Navy SEALs. For the first time, her voice broke.

"I didn't know those young men. I'm not a mother. Still, I can't imagine anything more painful than losing a son. When I called Jack Northern's mother today to offer my condolences, her tears broke my heart."

"Jack Northern? He was on that copter? He's dead?"

London burst into tears. Suddenly there was a hole in her heart that she couldn't imagine ever filling.

"I loved him," she said, startling Betty Edsel and Kameela Ishaad. "I loved him. I want to die."

Betty Edsel moved to the sofa beside London. She cradled her in her arms and pulled London's head to her chest. This hurts so much, she thought, trying to recall if she'd ever felt so much pain. Yet, in comforting this young woman, in feeling her pain, she also felt a sense of worth that long had eluded her. Was this what being a mother felt like?

CHAPTER 32

WEDNESDAY, APRIL 8
SOMEWHERE IN THE AIR OVER QATAR

The pilot announced they were thirty minutes away from their destination. Soon this Qatar Airlines flight would land in Doha, and John Edsel would have to make his move. He smiled nervously at the two Secret Service agents across the aisle. They both yawned, clearly as exhausted as Edsel by the seven thousand mile flight. Edsel hadn't wanted them to accompany him. But Jesse Grant had insisted. It didn't matter that John Edsel had resigned the Presidency. It didn't matter that he'd left office in disgrace. Grant had declared that the United States of America was still obligated to protect him, even though a majority of the population wanted Edsel Jones to disappear, if one believed the commentary on shows ranging from Fox on the right to MNBC on the left.

John Edsel wanted to disappear too. If he could duck these Secret Service clowns once he landed in Doha, he knew he could do it. Only an hour after the news of the Black Hawk crash went public, followed within minutes by the Bree Collard video, Edsel was on his computer transferring two million dollars from the bank account he shared with Betty, and another million from an account in the Canary Islands, to one he'd set up in Thailand. That gave him a total of three million dollars. One of the advantages of being married to a woman as wealthy as Betty was she didn't notice those annual transfers of a few hundred thousand or so that he'd been making from their joint account for the past few years. With that kind of cash in the bank, he could finally live the life he wanted, focused on pleasure instead of power, but only if he wasn't stalked by reporters and the Secret Service.

Edsel and the agents sailed through the airport, unencumbered by Immigration, Customs or Security. Even a disgraced former President of the United States commanded some important privileges. They hopped in a waiting limo and headed to the Four Seasons. Once they'd checked in, Edsel told the men to scatter. He needed some serious down time. He needed to decompress. He needed to pray. The men, who initially looked dubious, were impressed by that last invocation. They scurried off to their rooms, evidently believing Edsel's was a reasonable request. This trip had, in fact, been billed as a chance for the disgraced president to reflect alone on his misdeeds, although the truth was that Jesse Grant told him to leave or face indictment. Qatar struck many as an odd place for a contemplative retreat. The TV punsters had jokingly wondered how John Edsel would survive in a country without a casino, where liquor was illegal, and where most of the women still wore burkas. What they didn't know was that John Edsel had chosen Doha because it offered an easy connecting flight to Kuala Lumpur and from there to Phuket. With the layovers, there were at least two opportunities to shed his Secret Service minders on the way. After half an hour in his room, Edsel stepped back into the hotel hallway, dragging only a single rolling suit case behind him. On the sidewalk outside he grabbed a taxi. Within thirty minutes he was back at Doha International Airport, checking in, by himself, for the next flight to Kuala Lumpur.

Edsel spent a nervous hour in the airline terminal, the collar of his coat raised and the brim of his baseball cap lowered to hide his face. While that gimmick shielded the famous visage of the forty-sixth President of the United States from public view, Edsel worried that it would arouse suspicion. When he looked at himself in the bathroom mirror, he looked like the prototype of a mad bomber. No one seemed to pay him any mind, however. He boarded the Qatar Airlines flight at seven thirty and the flight took off as scheduled at eight. Five hours later he landed in Kuala Lumpur and effortlessly changed planes for Phuket. Edsel marveled that the trip had been so uneventful. He was impressed with himself for negotiating airports in countries he hadn't even heard of until he logged onto his computer to make the airline reservation. Thank God the State Department had insisted on getting him a passport, despite his well-publicized declaration that he was one President who never intended to leave the United States of America. Edsel tilted his first class seat back and, dipping into his the satchel under his seat, pulled out a handful of wrinkled and worn magazine pages from Hustler magazine. He'd spend the next half hour fantasizing about the life he'd live in Phuket. With three million dollars, he might even be able to buy one of those beer bars on Balang Road that opened to the sidewalk, with the girls who called out "hey handsome" to every man who walked by, inviting them in for a beer, and more. Imagine having a job peddling sex, something he knew and loved and, frankly, was good at, instead of peddling politics, where he'd always felt like a con artist on the verge of getting caught.

It was mid-afternoon as the small plane descended into Phuket. From his window seat, John Edsel could see the blue waters of Phang Nga Bay dotted with colorful fishing boat and dozens of green islands. He pushed his way through the crowded terminal, this time forced to pass through Immigration and Customs, flashing a passport that drew no untoward attention. He hailed a taxi and within fifteen minutes was at the front desk of the Patong Thai Guesthouse. The proprietor's attention, and that of half a dozen guests, was fixed on the television mounted high in the corner of the lobby. The image of Anderson Cooper was quickly replaced with Jesse Grant standing beyond a White House podium emblazoned with the Presidential seal, the same podium where only yesterday John Edsel, standing alone, had announced his resignation. Now it all seemed so distant, so foreign, so unbelievable really. For a second Edsel surveyed the rustic bamboo furniture in the lobby, glanced at the fan overhead, and then smiled at the cute Thai girl (maybe she was fifteen?) who looked so alluringly at him from the staircase. Had he really been President of the United States? It all seemed like a bizarre dream.

"Fellow citizens, I come before you today to share an important decision I've come to in the last twenty four hours, with the help of Almighty God." Jesse Grant paused and took a sip of water.

"I've asked the Federal Bureau of Investigation to examine what I believe has been a conspiracy to cover up the criminal misdeeds of John Edsel, a conspiracy that I believe extends to the highest levels of the Republican Party. My fellow citizens, I want to disavow as strongly as possible the sort of behavior that led John Edsel to resign from office, and to disavow as strongly as possible those who knew of his behavior and concealed it. To that end, as of this moment I resign from the Republican Party. I declare my allegiance to the Democratic Party, a party whose morals, whose core beliefs, align with mine and those of the majority of Americans. Also, I have requested the resignation of Lockehart Jones, the senior advisor to the former President, whose complicity is now under investigation. I have named as his replacement a former student and old friend from my days at Mississippi State University, Ahmed Abdul Azhar. Ladies and gentlemen, he is going to lead our mission to find and kill Abdullah bin-Salem."

The television cameras shifted quickly to the President's side, where a darkly handsome man in what looked to be an expensive suit offered a modest smile. At that, the television went dark, apparently the result of another interruption of Phuket's notoriously unreliable electrical system.

Edsel stood there, stunned at what he'd seen. His vice

president a Democrat? An FBI investigation? The proprietor looked even more stunned, if that were possible. Edsel couldn't imagine how this swarthy man in a Hawaiian shirt could have as much skin in the game of Washington politics as John Edsel. The proprietor shook his head, as if to clear his mind of what he'd just seen. Then he forced a smile and turned to Edsel.

The two men stared at one another quizzically, each seemingly trying to recall where they'd met. The realization came simultaneously. Each reached the same unspoken conclusion as to what to do about it.

"Greetings kind sir," Abdullah bin-Salem said, offering to shake Edsel's hand. "The United States, it is such an interesting country, is it not? My name is Abbie."

"It is indeed," said John Edsel. "But this is going to be my new home, and I hear it's damned interesting here too. My name is Johnnie. I'm pleased to meet you Abbie. If you're free later tonight, can I buy you a drink and get your advice on starting a business here?"

"I'd be delighted Johnnie," Abdullah said. "The bars on Balang Road don't get going until eleven o'clock. Come down to the lobby then and I'll show you around town."

As Edsel headed for his room, the bell on the check-in counter jingled and Abdullah moved quickly to greet a new guest — another American. He copied the man's passport and ran his credit card through the system. His business card read "Private Investigator, Mid-South Manufacturing."

"Welcome Mr. Tinsley," he said. "We're delighted to have you at Patong Thai."

Neal Tinsley only grunted as he took the key from Abdullah. Abdullah noticed a bulge on the right side of jacket. A pistol? Whatever, Abdullah thought. He had to get used to the fact that not all guests would be as amiable as Johnnie Edsel. He was looking forward to that drink.

CHAPTER 33

WEDNESDAY, APRIL 8
THE BOLAN PASS
THE TOBA KAKAR MOUNTAINS
PAKISTAN

Jack Northern looked at his watch, one of the few things that had survived the previous night's explosion. He had been walking for eight hours now, without food, without water, with no sense of where he was or where he was headed. It was enough, somehow, to know that he was putting distance between himself and the horrific pile of broken machinery and seared flesh at Abdullah bin-Salem's camp. Now, however, he could go no further. He was thirsty, exhausted, weak. He squatted at the side of the stone road on which he'd been walking. Enormous mountains, beige and barren, rose around him. The silence was deafening. Northern yearned for a sound, any sound, that would signal there was life around him.

So it had come to this. He would die here, his body likely undiscovered except by some hungry animal. His parents would never know for sure what became of the son for whom they held so much hope. He would never know what he could have become. Would he have left the Secret Service and practiced law? Would he have entered politics and government, taking what he had learned to help reform it? Would he have let himself succumb to the love, if it was love, that he felt for London Comfort? His was a story that would have no real end. Jack Northern closed his eyes and stretched his body out along the side of the road. The heat was unbearable. There was nothing more that he could do. The end, if not here, clearly was near. His only option was to wait for it.

It took all three men, barefoot and clad in dirty thawbs, to lift the body into the bed of the pickup truck. The man was long. He was heavy. From what remained of the uniform, this clearly was the body of a soldier, and an American at that. Anwar tilted the man's head forward, pushed his lips apart, and tried to pour some water from his canteen into his mouth. Hakim poured more water on his forehead. Jawad watched his sons. In a minute or two, the man moved slightly. Then he moaned. Anwar poured more water, and all three men dragged the man into a sitting position against the rear window of the truck. The man opened his eyes. He looked around. He was alive.

Jack Northern was dazed. Three Arab men were crouched around him, staring intently. One was offering a drink of water. Northern wondered if this effort to revive him would be followed by protracted torture and a beheading, filmed and distributed on the Internet to stir the faithful to action. Not that it mattered. He wasn't really alive. He was in another universe. He saw what was happening around him as through a telescope.

"You are American?" one man asked, in fractured English.

Northern nodded yes.

"You are dying," the man said. "You need help. You go with us."

###

It was cold and dark when Jack woke up. He was stretched out on a sandy piece of blanket, three or four feet from a flickering fire. Three men were clustered around the fire, roasting pieces of meat threaded on sticks. The men were speaking in Balochi, a language Northern didn't know but could recognize from his brief SEALs training. As he watched the men twirl the sticks through the fire, it dawned on him where he was, and that he still didn't know who these men were. Jack shifted his body and groaned in pain. A young man came over to him and offered him a canteen of water.

"Mister. How do you feel? the young man asked.

"I hurt everywhere," Jack replied. "At least I am alive. That is a good thing, I hope. But that is up to you. What are you going to do with me?"

"You are American, no?" the young man asked. "We are going to take you to Kandahar, to your people. They can take you to a hospital. You are badly injured mister."

"Thank you. I have to ask, why would you do this for me? I am a stranger, a foreigner, an American."

"And I am Anwar. I know your country. Until two years ago I drove a taxi in New York City. That is not why we are doing this. We are doing this because of my father," and here Anwar gestured to an elderly man sitting next to the fire. "We are doing this because my father knows you are someone's son."

"I am Jack. Jack Northern. I am grateful to your father. Does he speak English?"

"No sir. But I will tell him," said Anwar, who quickly translated Jack's expression of gratitude into Balochi. The old man smiled and nodded at Jack.

"My youngest brother, my father's son, he died on the road through this Bolan Pass. We found his body, with his leg and arm ripped off. He was killed by your drones."

"I am so sorry," Jack said. "I can't believe that you would rescue me if my country killed your brother."

"It is strange," Anwar said. "My brother and I think so. To be honest, if it were not for our father, we would kill you. We saw the pain our brother's death brought to our father and to our mother. Our father said he couldn't let another father, another mother, suffer the way they did."

Hakim brought Jack some cubes of broiled beef and draped another dusty blanket over him.

"Now you sleep," Anwar told Northern. "Tomorrow you will be on your way home."

Jack awoke the next morning to find three men lifting him into the back of their pickup truck. They covered him with a tarp, which Anwar explained would shield him from the view of those who might not share their father's feelings about rescuing injured Americans. Jack pulled the corner of the tarp back so that he could watch the landscape though which they passed. The trip would take six hours, Anwar had said. To Jack, it seemed more like twenty-four hours — twenty-four glorious hours. As they moved through the Pishin Valley, Jack watched acres of orchards float by, with trees bearing apples, grapes, peaches, and apricots. The green trees speckled with colorful fruit disappeared as the pickup truck rumbled toward the Khojak Pass. Steep copper red and russet mountains and cliffs rose on either side of the Pass, and Northern was almost blinded by the sun overhead until the truck entered a three-mile tunnel framed by two stone towers obviously erected in an earlier century. Soon they were moving through the Chaman Bypass approaching the Afghan border. Jack drifted in and out of consciousness on this journey. While awake, he marveled at the scenery around him. As he drifted into unconsciousness, he explored another unknown territory — the point, the purpose, the meaning of being Jack Northern. Now that it seemed likely he would live, now that he knew how closely death lurked, he had no excuse for not considering other ways to live his life. His model, he was surprised to realize, was London Comfort. She had led a famously shallow life, but, when she saw what was happening to Bree Collard, she did something about it, at no little risk to herself. Jack had spent little time with London, although he wasn't sure that hours spent together equated with knowledge and intimacy. John Edsel and Betty Evans were evidence of that. What he knew about London mattered more than what he didn't know — what sort of music she liked, what food she ate, her favorite color. He knew she was a woman capable of love, a woman capable of compassion, a woman who just might be willing to leave behind a life of celebrity for a life of meaning. If he lived long enough to return to Washington, she was the woman Jack Northern wanted to be with.

As they approached the Weesh crossing point at the Afghani border, the pickup truck took off on a bumpy detour, shaking Northern awake and sending ripples of pain through his body that reminded him just how badly damaged he was. They were avoiding the border checkpoint, Anwar explained, for fear they'd be stopped by the Afghani soldiers, known for their hatred of an America whose millions in funding they nevertheless eagerly accepted. An hour passed. Northern woke up, realizing the pickup truck no longer was moving. Someone yanked the tarp off his body. As Jack shielded his face from the blinding light he heard an American voice.

"Oh fuck! Who the hell is this?"

CHAPTER 34

WEDNESDAY, APRIL 22
THE FEDERAL SUITE
THE HAY-ADAMS HOTEL
WASHINGTON, DC

"No Roberto. No interviews. No TV. I don't care what people are thinking, what people are saying. Tell them London Comfort says, 'No comment'."

London tossed her cell phone onto the bed next to her Vuitton trunk, where Kameela was placing layer upon layer of clothing.

"There must be two hundred reporters and photographers down on the street," she said. "You're more famous than ever."

It was true that, in her brief career in Hollywood, London had never experienced the attention she was getting now. There were stories about her on the front pages of the New York Times, the Washington Post, the LA Times. Reporters were calling from the Times of London, from Le Monde in Paris. She was used to being on the TV gossip shows, but now Roberto was getting calls for interviews from CBS News, and CNN, and even Fox.

The London Comfort they were describing was nothing like the one she and her friends had created so many years ago. London found it interesting that, without benefit of an interview, they now portrayed her as an idealistic, intelligent, patriotic young woman whose biggest passion was saving other women from sexual abuse. Then again, maybe there was some truth in that. Back in high school, Betty and Rachel had always seen more in her than she had seen in herself. Even Betty Edsel described a London Comfort that was unfamiliar to her. She still remembered the First Lady's words: "curiosity and energy." Thankfully, the news coverage didn't include a hint of the sex tape Jason had made. Somehow Kameela had gotten her hands on it and destroyed what she claimed was the only copy.

""I'm famous, and the man I love is dead. So what good is fame Kameela? I just want to get out of this hotel and get back to LA. Can you believe we haven't even been here two months? It seems like a lifetime."

"But what are you getting back to London? What am I getting back to? We really haven't talked about that. It's great that the President got your sentence commuted. So you're not going back to jail. Where are you going then?"

London sat on the edge of the bed.

"I don't know Kameela. I really don't know. I do know where I'm not going. I'm not going back to the life I had before I got here. I'm not going back to Jason and that crowd. I'm not going back to a life as London Comfort, the dumb celebrity. I miss Jack, Kameela."

London started crying and reached out to hold Kameela's hand.

"Wherever I go, I hope you'll go with me. I'm going to need security now, more than ever. I'm going to need someone beside me who knows what I've gone through and what I've been struggling with."

"Wherever you go, London, I'll be with you."

The two women hugged.

"Now let's get these damned trunks packed so we can get out of here," London said. "We have to be at the airport in four hours. We're going to have to figure out a way to get through those damned reporters. I'm going to do a take a look in the sitting room to make sure we haven't forgotten anything there."

London stepped into the sitting room and heard a knock at the door. She was puzzled. They hadn't ordered room service. The bed already had been made, and the rooms had been cleaned hours earlier. London looked through the peephole in the door. All she could make out was a tall figure, a man, with his head tilted away so that she couldn't see who he was. Well, she could take care of this. If it was a pushy journalist, Kameela was there to offer back up.

From the bedroom, Kameela heard the door to the Federal Suite open. Then she heard a loud scream. She ran into the sitting room, her pistol drawn from her burka. She looked on, amazed, as a man, his head bandaged and his arm in a cast, dropped to his knees in front of London. London's cries, Kameela now realized, were of happiness and not fear.

"London, will you marry me?

"Oh yes, Jack. Oh yes, oh yes, oh yes."

London fell to her knees to hug Jack. Kameela stepped back and closed the door.

Henry E. Scott

CHAPTER 35

SATURDAY, APRIL 25
DIPLOMATIC RECEPTION ROOM
THE WHITE HOUSE, WASHINGTON, DC

A footman pulled open the door to the Diplomatic Reception Room. London stepped in, more nervous, more excited, and happier than she had ever been. She cradled a bouquet of long-stemmed, wine-colored calla lilies that perfectly complemented the demure pink dress she and Kameela had purchased on her first weekend in Washington. Standing in front of her was a justice of the peace who Betty Edsel had hurriedly summoned for the occasion. The rows of chairs on either side of the room were filled with co-workers who London Comfort had come to regard as friends. Sitting at the front, where a bride's mother and father would be, were President Jesse Grant and Betty Edsel, who had agreed to serve as the unmarried president's First Lady. And there was Jack Northern, smiling and looking as nervous as London felt. Tufts of blond hair poked through the bandage around his head. His arm was still in a cast, necessitating the removal of one sleeve of his suit. London had never seen a department store suit look so good. Her friends rose and smiled as she made her way to the front of the room. She turned and handed her bouquet to Kameela, who in her black burka was London's bridesmaid.

The vows were simple and nondenominational, to accommodate Jack's Catholicism and London's lack of religion. After each offered an "I do," Jack slipped a ring onto London's hand. The kiss that followed washed away all her nervousness, all her doubts. This was the man for her.

At the small reception afterwards in the Family Dining Room, London was handed a card. Opening it, she read a message from her father, who had been in China when he got the news of his daughter's impending wedding and couldn't return in time.

"I wish my little girl all the happiness in the world. My only regret is that I can't be there to see you wed the man you love."

London's mother hadn't responded to the news of her daughter's wedding. Then again, as Betty Edsel gave her a hug, London realized for the first time that it might be possible to choose one's mother and father. She loved the father she had. If she had to make a choice, why not choose as a mother a woman who admired her and told her so, a woman who had saved her life, a woman who had been there for her during one of the most painful moments a young woman could endure?

As Betty Edsel stepped aside, London noticed half a dozen young women, all White House co-workers, gathered around Kameela to ask questions about her burka. She grabbed the bouquet of calla lilies off the table and hurled it in their direction. The young women stepped back to watch the wine-colored flowers sail in a graceful arc. It landed squarely in the outstretched hands of a smiling Kameela Ishaad, and the room resounded with cheers and applause.

ABOUT THE AUTHOR

Henry E. Scott is the author of "Shocking True Story: The Rise and Fall of Confidential, 'America's Scandalous Scandal Magazine'," (Pantheon, 2009). Scott is a former journalist and media business executive who has worked at the Raleigh Times, the Charlotte Observer, the Hartford Courant and The New York Times. He was president and editorial director of Out magazine and publisher of Metro New York, a New York City free daily newspaper aimed at young people. A native of North Carolina and a graduate of the University of North Carolina at Chapel Hill, he now lives in West Hollywood, California.